LOBO CORONADO

AND THE

LEGACY OF THE WOLF

by

Manuel Ruiz[3]

Copyright © 2017 Manuel Ruiz[3]

All rights reserved.

Cover by Elartwyne Estole

ISBN: 0998448605
ISBN-13: 978-0998448602

DEDICATION

For my parents,
Rosie and Manuel, Jr.
and my brothers, Marc and Matthew.
We were fortunate to have grown up in a
house filled with love and laughter.
It wasn't always perfect, but it was home.
Thank you, Mom and Dad, for making it possible.
Love you all.

CONTENTS

	Acknowledgments	i
1	Night Shadows	1
2	An Invitation	5
3	A Kindly Frenemy	11
4	New Beginnings	15
5	Crystal Clear	23
6	A Visual Bloodline	31
7	The Freaksome Threesome	41
8	Amigos	51
9	Virtual Fighter	57
10	The Call	65
11	Bay Watch	73
12	A Rude Awakening	89
13	Family Connections	99
14	Texas Trouble	111
15	Examination	131
16	Detective	141
17	Workaround	155
18	An Eye for Truth	167
19	Final Arrival	175
20	Meet and Greet	181
21	A Royal Battle	187
22	Resolutions	197

ACKNOWLEDGMENTS

Thanks to the following:

My first critique group: Varian Johnson and Karl Staib
Dr. Lila Guzman
Austin Chapter of the SCBWI

My High School English Teachers, who went above & beyond for a student who loved to read and tell stories:
Rudy Salazar, Peggy France and Martha Westfall

Special thanks to my Goddaughter Alaina,
for inspiring my favorite character.

To my family, thank you for being my center
and making me whole.
Daisy, Kristopher & Austin

I once asked my son, Kristopher, what kind of character he would like me to create. Although this character didn't have a name or story yet, that was the day Lobo Coronado was born.

CHAPTER ONE: NIGHT SHADOWS

"Please don't kill me!" Lobo screamed as his legs moved faster than he ever knew they could.

Lobo slipped on the sidewalk and landed on his stomach. He felt his heart slam against the concrete with each beat.

The whispers from above grew louder.

"Coronado... son..." was all he could make out.

He scanned the ground and picked up a baseball-sized rock. He jumped up, turned and raised his hand.

"Don't make me throw this," he yelled.

No one was behind him.

"Smells... like Coronado," the voices were clearer now.

Lobo looked up and saw a black cloud drifting low, camouflaged by the night sky. Dark shadows moved within the cloud. Lobo threw the rock, but it didn't come close to hitting anything. He turned and ran, but after two steps his side slammed into something.

He turned and the head of a Doberman was hanging

over the fence. The dog growled, revealing his fangs.

His bark made Lobo jump back.

A screen door slammed open.

"I see you," a voice said. "You stay away from my Killer B!"

Mr. Kindly was the neighbor all the kids were afraid of, but Lobo had more things to fear tonight.

B's head turned upwards and he started barking at the cloud, which floated back and away from the attention. Lobo didn't hesitate and darted away.

It was an hour past bed check at Muckingdale Academy, but Lobo was able to get back in through the same window with the loose lock he used so often before. He was usually quiet, but his hands were shaking and the window rattled as he pulled it up. He jumped through and landed on the carpet. Lobo looked up, but no one was around. He snuck back through the hallway and towards his room, number 7, which was second to the last on the right.

He turned the knob slowly. A ten-year-old boy with brown hair and chicken legs protruding through his long shorts was sitting on his bed.

"Hey, Kyle," Lobo said, trying to catch his breath.

"You took way too long, this time, Lobo," Kyle said. "I told the headmaster you were in the bathroom and he almost went looking for you."

Lobo pulled a candy bar from his back pocket and gave it to his roommate.

"I made it to the store, but something was chasing me. I think I lost it."

"What do you mean something was chasing you?"

Lobo hesitated, but Kyle was his closest friend.

"I think a cloud was chasing me. It was dark and there were voices. I think they were saying my name."

Kyle's eyes bulged. "Voices? You don't think they'll

come in here, do you? I told you not to go out again."

"Yeah, maybe sneaking out three times this week was pushing it. I can't explain it, but I keep thinking something's gonna happen."

"I think a black cloud chasing you counts as something happening," Kyle said.

The ground started shaking. The walls vibrated and doors banged.

"Is this an earthquake?" Kyle was trembling.

"I'm not sure. Let's get out of here."

Lobo pulled Kyle out of the bed and they ran into the hallway. Boys were running everywhere. They followed the crowd to the common room, which was the center of the Academy where all the dorm hallways met. Glass broke as a loud wind whisked by their heads.

"What was that?" Kyle yelled.

"The shadows, I think. Go hide by the headmaster's office door where there aren't any windows."

Kyle rushed to the door and crouched against it. Lobo stood in the middle of the building, looking up at the vaulted ceiling.

A strong gust of wind spun near the front doors and formed a small funnel that bounced around the room. Lobo jumped behind a couch in the sitting area. The mini-twister blasted by Kyle, blowing the door open and Kyle through it.

Lobo jumped from his hiding spot and toward the room.

"Kyle!"

He ran inside and Kyle was on the ground. The twister was gone.

A dark shadow darted across the room. Lobo's eardrums vibrated with the sound of a fly buzzing inside his head.

The noise grew louder and started to sound like a radio with bad reception. Lobo dashed back out of the office and across the main hall where boys were scrambling around frightened as more funnels formed.

Lobo stopped and doubled over, grasping the sides of his head as the vibrations pierced through him. Then the buzzing started to speak.

"Jer-e-mi-ah Coro-nado. . ."

"What?" Lobo yelled.

"Are you. . . son of Sebastian?"

"Yes, Sebastian was my fath--"

The shadows converged on Lobo and enveloped him, forming a black cloud. It rose into the air and then shot through the large front windows, shattering more glass as it whooshed Lobo away from the Academy and into the night sky.

CHAPTER TWO:
AN INVITATION

Lobo woke up with a low humming noise in his head. He realized he was alone in the dark, sitting on a cold, steel chair. He saw two open doors to each side. He stood up, but lost his balance and fell back into his seat.

"Jeremiah Coronado," a coarse voice echoed in the room. "You are safe."

Lobo checked the room, but only saw a big aquarium filled with bubbling water and a few unusual looking fish. One was bright purple and had three green eyes. Another had no tail and a small red one looked like it had a hairy beard.

"Am I a prisoner?" Lobo asked.

"No. You are free to leave anytime you please."

Lobo shrugged and tried to stand up again. He shuffled slowly toward one of the doors. A dark shadow, the same kind that swept him up at the Academy, appeared and moved in front of the door.

"Free?" Lobo tried to step by the shadow, but it didn't budge. "Sure feels like I'm a prisoner."

"Hear me out," said the voice.

Lobo hesitated a moment, then returned to his seat.

"I have been waiting for the right time to contact you, Jeremiah."

Lobo's eyebrows rose. "It's Lobo. And why should I listen?"

Mechanical sounds of shifting gears, scratching metal and electronic beeps came from behind the aquarium.

A black and green object emerged that looked like a futuristic go-cart with wings. The sides were rounded and the vehicle hovered in the air over a white fog. It turned and a figure twisted, then rose from the box. Lobo first saw a man's head followed by shoulders and torso. Thin tubes and wires were hooked up to the man's chest. The box shifted closer, revealing an older man with long, silver hair. He stared at Lobo with squinted eyes. The man's body elevated higher and he appeared to be sitting up. He had a long nose and face, but aside from his body, there were no normal limbs. There was loud popping as two mechanical arms and hands shot out of the box's sides.

Lobo jumped out of his seat. "What are. . ."

"Don't be afraid. I lost my limbs, liver, kidneys and a lung a few years ago, but fourteen surgeries and this hover chair have allowed me to survive."

"What happened?"

The man grunted. "No more questions. Now, you listen."

Lobo wanted to run, but he couldn't keep his eyes off of the man and his machine.

"I know who your parents are and what happened to them. You were orphaned at the age of five. Your mother and father were killed in a fire, which you barely escaped, and you've been living at the Academy ever since."

Lobo's chest tightened. "I already know what

happened to my parents, but what's it to you?"

"I know some things about your family that you don't. Interrupt me again and I may not tell you another word, which is something I expect you will regret. May I continue?"

Lobo sat back in his chair.

"Your mother was a special woman. By special, I mean not exactly human."

Lobo opened his mouth but decided that the risk of not hearing more wasn't worth it and snapped his jaws shut.

The man continued. "Your father was a police detective. A general job description, but you knew this, correct?"

"Yes."

"He was known as the Grey Wolf. He could attack and subdue a criminal in the darkest of nights and disappear so fast that no one remembered seeing his face. He wasn't just great at what he did. He was the best. Your nickname, Lobo, came from your father's own nickname. Lobo is the Spanish word for wolf."

The man pointed his mechanical hand at Lobo's chest. "Do you still have the medallion?"

Lobo reached inside his shirt and pulled out a silver charm and necklace. The medallion was the face of a wolf with eyes made of blue, multi-cut stones. Even in the dark room, the eyes glistened.

"The eyes of the wolf glow in pure darkness, don't they?"

Lobo remembered the times he was almost caught sneaking out because of the blue glow and nodded.

"The rock that forged the eyes on your amulet is not of this Earth. It comes from another world. Through an unusual assignment and a chance encounter, your father accidentally ended up in this realm, which was where he met your mother. They were as different as their homelands, but they made it work. They married against the wishes of their closest friends and family. There were consequences from this marriage, some of which I believe led to their deaths."

Lobo sat at the edge of his seat as his hands clasped the armrests.

A mechanical arm reached into the hovering chair and pulled up a metal cup. The old man took a long sip. "Jeremiah, I know much more about your family, but now is not the time to discuss history. What's important is that you know I have this information and am willing to provide more, but I need you to do something first, and it must be done willingly."

Lobo fell back into his seat. "So I don't get any more information until I do what you want?"

"I know you have more questions, but things must happen in the proper order. There is a woman named Alina you must meet who will help make more sense of what I've told you. To reach her, you will need to speak with your neighbor, the one with the dog."

"Mr. Kindly?" Lobo asked.

"Yes, Kindly. You must see him."

"But he hates me. He hates all kids and sends his dog after us."

"When I discovered your location," the old man said, "I bought that house. Mr. Kindly works for me and had been keeping watch over you while I healed. About a year ago, when I was finally strong enough, I came to the house to observe you. Based on recent events, I felt it was finally time to make contact. I want you to return to Kindly and show him your medallion. Tell him the Zaan has begun and you must see Alina. He'll tell you how to find her."

"What's the Zaan?"

"You'll know soon enough."

Lobo massaged his lip with the knuckle of his index finger, weighing his options. "Why should I trust you?"

"You have no reason to. I can only entice you with the hope of knowing more about your parents. Now, my Shadow Guards will take you to Kindly's house."

"What about the Academy?"

"I will speak to your headmaster. It's time to go."

The two shadows that were guarding the doors whisked toward Lobo and started to envelop him again.

Before disappearing, Lobo heard the old man's voice. "Jeremiah, when you meet Alina, be sure to tell her that your grandfather sent you."

CHAPTER THREE: A KINDLY FRENEMY

The shadow cloud left Lobo across the street from Kindly's house. As the cloud disappeared, Lobo noticed the sun was peeking over the horizon. He had been gone all night.

He sped across the street. Killer B was waiting and broke into a barking frenzy. Lobo stood several feet from the fence but made no effort to hide.

The front door of the house flew open and Mr. Kindly stuck his head out. "Boy, you ready to be dog food? Not feeling too bright today?"

Lobo didn't answer. Instead, he walked straight to the fence gate, reached into his shirt and held his medallion in the air. His hands were shaking as the wolf's eyes glowed. Killer B stopped barking.

"What do you have there?" Mr. Kindly asked.

"I was told you would know."

Mr. Kindly let his door slam shut and he took a few steps on his porch. "You need to come over here, Lobo Coronado."

Lobo reached for the fence gate, but he hesitated as he made eye contact with Killer B.

"He won't harm you."

Lobo unlatched the gate and took small steps up the cobblestone path, never turning his back on B. He stepped over a large rock and tripped.

Killer B growled as he tried to get up.

By the time he raised his head, the dog was facing him with sharp fangs exposed. Lobo was too frightened to yell, but he gasped as B playfully licked his face.

"All bark that one. Now come here."

Lobo got up and wiped his face on his sleeve. He reached the porch and showed Mr. Kindly the amulet.

"Do you know where this came from?" Mr. Kindly asked.

"I just know it wasn't made on Earth. I'm supposed to tell you I need to see Alina, and that something called the Zaan has begun."

Mr. Kindly got in Lobo's face. "Who told you this?"

"He didn't tell me his name, but he said he's my grandfather. He's an old man living in a hovering machine and says you work for him. He kidnapped me last night."

"Kidnapped? Is that what all that ruckus was?" Mr. Kindly shook his head. "What else did he tell you?"

"That you've been watching over me."

"Yeah, the job of a lifetime. I guess I did something right. You still have all your fingers and toes. Let's not waste any more time. Come on, then."

Lobo followed Mr. Kindly and Killer B around the house. The backyard was filled with more than twenty small gardens, each with different types of flowers.

Mr. Kindly pointed a finger. "Go inside."

"Where?" Lobo asked. "In the rose garden?"

"No, in the doghouse."

THE LEGACY OF THE WOLF

A wooden doghouse stood in the center of the backyard, right next to a garden of giant sunflowers. It was painted bright orange and had the name Killer B written in large red letters on both sides of its slanted roof.

"How am I supposed to fit in there?"

Mr. Kindly grunted. "Just crawl in."

Lobo wasn't sure whether to trust this man he had feared for so long. Killer B lifted one paw, pointed his nose straight to his house and barked once.

Lobo walked toward the doghouse, got on his knees and stuck his head in. He saw a dirty blanket, a baseball and a raggedy doll without any arms or legs, which made him think of the old man who claimed to be his grandfather.

Mr. Kindly groaned. "You have to go all the way in."

Lobo squeezed in further.

"When you get there, tell them you are to speak with Alina only. Just show them the wolf."

Lobo struggled to turn his head and started to yell, "What's so. . ." but the door was gone.

The eyes of the wolf medallion glowed in the pitch black doghouse and a white light flashed, emitting a sharp squeal.

Lobo wailed as blue sparks flared and stung his body.

CHAPTER FOUR:
NEW BEGINNINGS

Lobo heard a bang and the flash of light left him seeing bright spots for a few seconds. Once the spots disappeared, his eyes adjusted and he was sitting at the bottom of a hill covered with the brightest green and yellow grass he had ever seen.

He stepped slowly up the hill and reached the top. Below, cow-like creatures grazed in the distance. Further down, someone was sitting near some trees and it looked like he was writing.

Lobo stepped softly towards the person but stopped as he got a better look at the cows. They were the same body shape and had the same thin tails as a normal cow, but they had two mouths and their ears reached down to just above the grass.

He looked back at the person taking notes to see if he noticed these deformed cows, but whoever it was kept on writing. Lobo walked closer and then crouched down. The thing that was writing wasn't a person at all.

The creature sat against a blue tree stump, writing into

a notepad with two thin sticks. Lobo moved closer to get a better look, but the creature didn't seem to notice. It wore the writing tool on the first two of its four fingers. As the first stick completed a word, the second finger leapt back over the first and started the next one. Lobo had never seen anyone write so fast before. He tried to step closer, but slipped and fell to his hands and knees.

The startled creature yelped. The writing sticks flew up and a piece of parchment floated down near Lobo. It had a long line that ran off the page. The creature jumped up and flipped around.

They stared at each other for a few moments. The creature wore a fleece-like jacket with raised collars and had a thin body and larger head with ears that pointed up like a bat.

"Are you hurt?" it asked.

Lobo's eyes moved toward it, but he didn't respond.

"Can you speak? You look like an Earth being, but I haven't seen many of you. You could be a dog, or a. . . weasel, I think they're called." The creature dropped on all fours like Lobo and barked. No response.

"I'm. . . not a dog," Lobo said.

"Wonderful, I was afraid you might bite me if you were. You are a human boy then?"

"Yes. Who, I mean what, are you?"

The creature combed through spiky hair and stroked the tips of his ears. "Am I really that unusual? I mean, haven't you seen something like me on Earth?"

Lobo shook his head. "The claws and fangs are a little scary."

"I'm a vampire," the creature said. "My name is Vonqua Desanger Vampiere."

"Vonka Dessinger Vampie," Lobo said.

The vampire laughed. "Vampie? I like the way that

sounds." He offered his hand to help the visitor to his feet.

Lobo took it and stood up. "I'm Lobo. Please don't suck my blood."

Vampie's face shriveled and he stuck out a pointed tongue. "Human blood? What a revolting thought. I've heard your kind tastes like rotten milk."

Lobo's head tilted. "You don't eat humans?"

"Not at all. I feed on animals, like the corna grazing over there, just long enough to satisfy my thirst and would never harm them." Vampie reached down and picked up his parchment and writing sticks. He stuffed them into a small pouch and strapped it on his back.

"What are those things you were writing with?" Lobo asked.

"Those are my Finger Quills. They are the most efficient writing tools available but are a difficult skill to master. I have been practicing for over two hundred years and still consider myself little more than a beginner. They are. . . Wait. What are you doing here?"

"I'm supposed to see someone," Lobo began as he looked Vampie up and down, "or some thing, named Alina."

Vampie's eyes widened. "Alina? She's the Queen of this world. I can tell you where to find her."

"What world is this?"

"This is Osidian."

A light popped over Vampie's shoulder and buzzed in high-pitched tones. Vampie replied with the same sounds.

"What was that?" Lobo asked as the light disappeared.

"A Sprite. I think Earthlings would call it a fairy. This one brought me a message. It seems that Queen Alina already knows you are here and I'm supposed to take you to her. I'm not sure why, but I'm not one to argue the wishes of my leader."

Vampie led Lobo on foot. "It's not far, and I'm sure you'll enjoy some of the scenery."

They passed the hill and more herds of cornas. They reached a line of fifty-foot trees that Vampie identified as garla trees.

Lobo's mouth fell open as he looked above the trees and saw more than twenty flying creatures in the air.

"Those are way too big to be birds," Lobo said.

Vampie smiled. "These are training grounds."

"Training for what?"

"Flying. There are a few races of winged beings native to Osidian. Come, let's move closer so you can get a better look."

They neared a clearing among the trees but still stayed back. A small audience sat in grass as thick as shaggy carpet while several instructors ran their students through flying drills.

"Most of the instructors are Rayjan," Vampie explained. "They have thick wings and are the strongest fliers. They're also easy to spot if you're not sure. See that instructor flying backward?"

Lobo saw an instructor that looked like he was doing backstrokes. He could hear the wind whoosh with each backward thrust. His wings were mixed with yellow and green feathers that almost glowed. He noticed others with multicolored wings.

"Only the Rayjans have colored wings?"

"Yes, they're visible even on the darkest of nights."

"What about the others?" Lobo asked. "The ones with white wings are either thinner or way smaller."

"Yes, those are two other flying races. The Eliria are the taller beings with shorter wingspans. They're fast but weak. The smaller ones with the rounder faces are the Cherubim. It takes time for them to develop their wings and to get them strong enough for flight."

"Can we watch for a minute?" Lobo asked.

"Just for a moment," Vampie said. "I don't want to delay our Queen any longer than necessary."

Lobo sat and listened.

"Time for strengthening drills," an instructor said.

The students were broken into four groups and were trying to fly straight up while carrying round weights. A small Cherub was having trouble carrying the ball in her hands.

"Keep trying, Gira," her instructor said. "You'll get it."

"I'm trying, Joran," the young Cherub said. She spread her small wings, but couldn't move any higher.

Another instructor was flying from group to group, overseeing progress. He flew next to Gira with his arms crossed. "Having trouble?"

"She's almost there, Kai," Joran said.

"She needs a different kind of encouragement," Kai argued. He flew toward a box of weighted objects on the ground and pulled out a few more balls.

"The problem is you need some incentive," Kai yelled as he headed back toward Gira. "Joran, take the weight from her."

"What are you going to do?" he asked.

Kai grabbed Joran's shoulder. "Who's the lead instructor and strongest flier on this realm?"

"You know you are."

"Then just do what I say."

Joran took the ball from the student.

Kai raised the ball and smiled. "Gira, catch this."

He tossed the ball hard to the Cherub. She caught it but struggled to stay in the air.

Kai crossed his arms and shook his head. "Do you want to fall?"

"It's too heavy," Gira said.

"Keep it together or you're going to hit the ground."

Joran tried to take one of the balls from Kai. "That's enough."

Kai pushed him back. "Not yet. Drop it, Gira."

"What is that guy's problem?" Lobo asked. He started to stand up.

"Don't interfere, Lobo," Vampie said. "If anyone recognizes you're not an Osidianite, you might bring on unwelcome attention."

He sat back down.

Gira let the ball fall and regained her balance.

Without saying a word, Kai threw another ball toward her. It hit her in the stomach before she could catch it and she plummeted backward, straight into the bright red leaves of a garla tree. Her shoulder cracked as it hit the blue bark.

Kai laughed. "Get back up. It's the only way you'll get this right."

Joran flew down to help.

"Is bullying girls what you need to feel important?" a girl's voice yelled from the crowd. Lobo saw a Cherub with brown, curly hair step forward. She wore a white sundress with a set of small wings protruding from her back. Her lips were pursed and her fists were clenched by her sides.

Kai flipped around and found the protester.

"Devon," he said as he shook his head. "I should have known."

"Joran was doing fine with her," Devon said. "You just did that for fun."

"Devon, Devon," Kai began, "I know this is just frustration from not being able to use your... well, I guess you'd call them wings, although they look more like they belong on a stunted coral bee." Kai spread his wings to their full width as he taunted her.

Some of the crowd started to laugh.

Devon cracked her knuckles. "If I could fly, I'd tag you so hard with one of those balls you'd cry like a newborn Sprite looking for its mommy."

"Is that so, little one? You don't have to fly to play target practice. Here."

Kai zoomed a ball in Devon's direction. She snatched it out of the air with one hand.

"I'll give you three chances," Kai said.

"I just need one, you arrogant crow," Devon said.

The Cherub's face turned redder with each word as she held the ball behind her back. She cupped it with both hands and several children sitting nearby gasped as it started to glow orange.

"Any time now," Kai said. "I'm getting bored."

Devon faked a throw, causing Kai to spin around. As soon as his back was turned, she snapped her arm forward and the ball hit Kai dead center on his back, shattering and spraying white powder.

He barely flinched. "Is that all you have, Devon? I'm disappointed. That wasn't even good enough to. . ."

Kai's wings wilted and he fell out of the air, smacking into the ground. The spectators, students, Lobo and even some of the instructors cheered.

"You enchanted the ball," Kai groaned. "You aren't supposed to perform spells on the training grounds."

He stood up to chase her, but lost his balance and fell sideways. He tried to extend his wings, but they crumpled even more.

Devon crossed her arms and stood tall. "It's a salt bomb, Kai. Remember that next time you feel like pushing me."

Two tiny balls of light appeared at Devon's sides and

buzzed wildly around her head.

Devon shrugged. "I knew you Sprites would show. It was worth whatever punishment I get this time." She grinned as she followed her escorts through the parade of cheers and applause.

CHAPTER FIVE:
CRYSTAL CLEAR

"We'd better move on," Vampie said. "That probably wasn't a great introduction to our world."

"Are you kidding me? That was cool. That Cherub was brave to stand up to that arrogant jerk."

"Maybe so, but let me assure you that most of our citizens are much more reasonable."

They continued on their way. Lobo saw Sprites flying in and out of several holes burrowed into a hillside. They passed tiny homes built of a crystal material. Some stood alone while others formed mini-neighborhoods.

"What other types of creatures live here?" Lobo asked.

"There are many. Your world's intelligent creatures are limited to humans, apes and a few water creatures that you can't communicate with. That is still true, correct?"

"I read that there are some people who can talk to chimps with sign language. We still can't talk to the dolphins yet, though."

"Here, we have multiple languages, but most of us understand each other. We have several races, such as the

Sprites and Fliers you've already seen, which make up our world."

Lobo wanted to ask about everything, but the new beings and surroundings overwhelmed him.

"We're almost there," Vampie said.

They walked up a larger hill. There were no more homes or beings around. As they walked further up the hill, a heavy fog covered the ground. Vampie stopped a few yards later.

"Ready?" Vampie asked.

"For what?"

Vampie pointed upward. "To go to the High Council. Just one more step."

Lobo looked up and then back at Vampie. "What step?"

Vampie's face turned red. "My deepest apologies, Lobo. I forgot that you must first be granted sight."

"Sight?"

"Yes. Just trust me for now."

Vampie stepped up and stood on the fog. He took another step in midair and motioned for Lobo to follow. Lobo stepped up and back down three times before shifting his weight onto the unseen surface. He almost lost his balance, but righted himself and stood next to Vampie.

They rose. Lobo felt like he was in a high-speed invisible elevator. His stomach twisted and he closed his eyes. His hand grabbed onto Vampie's thin shoulder and he dug in deeper with each passing second.

Vampie yelped. "Are you okay, Lobo?"

"Yes," he replied, keeping his eyes shut tight. "I'm just a little freaked out."

They stopped after a few moments, but Lobo didn't move.

"We're here. You can let go now." Vampie peeled Lobo's fingers off his shoulder.

Lobo opened his eyes, looked down and saw only air between his feet and the ground far below, then snapped them shut again. A moment later he heard the same high pitched gibberish as before and eased one eye open. Vampie was speaking to a cluster of Sprites.

"The Sprites are going to grant you sight," Vampie said.

The fairy creatures converged on Lobo and circled him.

Vampie patted him on the arm and stepped back. "Just let it happen. It might be disorienting."

Two Sprites flew into each of Lobo's eyes and emitted a golden particle spray. Lobo grunted as he was blinded, but kept still. The remaining three Sprites rushed into his chest and penetrated his heart.

Lobo heaved in and caught his breath. Once his eyes focused, he realized he was standing on a stairway, surrounded by crystal columns that blurred into the clouds above.

Vampie led Lobo up the wide stairs. Two large doors opened as they approached. Two tall, chrome-skinned beings stepped in front of them.

"These are Sentraelian Guards," Vampie said. "Just a security check."

A guard pressed his hand on Lobo's chest. The hand had three fingers and they let out a soft humming noise as each digit tapped slowly against him.

"The human is clear. You may proceed to the High Council chamber."

The pair entered a long hallway in a room that was twelve stories high. The floor and walls were covered in a smooth material that Lobo thought looked like a mix of crystal and marble, yet with each step, he felt as if he were walking on pillows.

"What is that bright crystal stuff?" Lobo asked.

"It's called crystalline," Vampie explained. "It's used in

many building materials on our realms."

The pair moved through the hall for several more yards until they reached a large wall and hit a dead end.

"What do we do now?" Lobo asked.

"We go to the next floor."

Lobo looked up and saw a platform more than forty feet above them, but didn't see any visible doors or stairs to reach it. Vampie checked the ground and then eased his foot on part of the floor, which contained multiple geometric designs, and a diamond-shaped step rose and snapped underneath his foot. Lobo took his lead and lifted his foot over another diamond pattern. He jumped as the piece snapped out. Vampie and Lobo rose to the top of the platform. They were lifted just above the next floor and stepped off their transports. Unlike the barren entrance, this area was filled with people, art and sculptures.

Lobo was greeted with stares, but he was studying the art around him and barely noticed.

"Who are the people in the statues?" Lobo asked. "They're so different."

"They are leaders and significant figures of our realms." Vampie pointed to one of the larger statues. "This is Cimball who united our realms. Earth does the same with their significant leaders as well, don't they?"

"Yes, we do. How do you know so much about Earth?"

"I read whatever I can about the different worlds, but Earth is one of the more fascinating places."

A being whose face was smooth as glass gave Lobo a gentle nod. Lobo started to wave back and realized more than a few people were looking in his direction. "Why is everyone staring?"

"Humans are highly uncommon. Even with so many different beings on our world, you stand out."

"How do they know? A lot of them look human."

"Earthlings give off a distinct scent and your clothing is a big giveaway."

Lobo looked at his feet. "I wish they'd stop."

"I understand, but imagine the reaction if I were to walk down your street?"

Lobo cracked a half-smile. "Yeah, people would probably do more than stare."

"The High Council chamber is just ahead," Vampie said. "They are conducting a public forum right now. I should give you a quick lesson in etiquette."

"Etiquette?"

"The procedures for addressing the council. First, do not speak until you are first asked a direct question and do not approach the council until they acknowledge you."

"Should I bow?" Lobo asked.

"No, nothing that formal. You may speak freely, but just be respectful."

"Okay, anything else?"

Vampie shook his head. "No, that's about it. If you're not sure about something, just look at me and I'll try and guide you."

They entered through a doorway that was over twenty feet high. The room's ceiling was more than eight stories tall and was filled with several hundred citizens. Eight thick columns, each painted with faces that Lobo recognized as some of the leaders from the statues he had seen earlier, towered from top to bottom. There was one other floor above them with seats and railings where more people were viewing the proceedings. Bright colored strips of thick cloth held together by crystalline ropes hung from the center of the pointed roof. Each long flag waved as if it were flying against a gentle wind, creating a soothing atmosphere within the chamber.

The crowd was fixated toward the front of the room

where seven seats, one large throne in the center surrounded by three smaller ones on each side, stood on a raised platform. A thin woman with hazel eyes and black hair bundled behind her head sat on the throne. Even seated she towered above those next to her. She was addressing someone on the floor and stopped every few moments to discuss with those around her. As Lobo moved closer, he noticed that what he first thought was just a white piece of her clothing surrounding her neck was actually a pair of feathered wings.

The woman was speaking to a snout-nosed creature that kept cracking his spiny fingers. The woman stopped in mid-sentence as she noticed Vampie approaching. She raised her hand and the snout-nose stepped back. The congregation grew quieter as they scrambled to get a look at their visitor.

"Queen Alina," Vampie began, "I present the Earthling known as Lobo."

"Vonqua the Vampire," Alina said. "I thank you for bringing him here. You may step forward, child."

Vampie nudged Lobo forward.

Alina studied his face. "Do you have the medallion?"

Lobo pulled his necklace from underneath his shirt and held it up. The wolf's eyes glowed brighter than usual. The other six council members burst into whispered conversations.

Alina addressed the entire room. "Citizens, the Earth child before me introduced as Lobo has a name that may be familiar. His birth name is Jeremiah Coronado."

The crowd gasped as Alina refocused on Lobo.

"Lobo, it is an honor to meet you. I am Alina of the Elidian race and head of the High Council of the Seven Tribes. Welcome to my home realm of Osidian."

Lobo moved closer and extended his hand. Alina

paused for a second and then shook it.

"I had forgotten about the customary human greeting," Alina said. "You may be surprised to know that the last person that greeted me this way was also named Coronado."

Lobo's eyebrows rose. "My father was here?"

"Yes, but before we discuss him or anything else, I would like to hear the message you bring."

Lobo cleared his throat. He felt like he was giving an oral book report in English class. "The Zaan has begun."

The room went silent.

"How do you know this and do you know what it means?" Alina asked.

"I have no idea what it means. A man who says he's my grandfather told me to deliver the message."

Alina pondered for a few moments.

"I have much to tell you, Lobo. I'm sure you'd like to know who we are and why you were sent here."

Lobo nodded.

"The High Council requests privacy." Alina's voice echoed throughout the room. Without a single protest, the crowd backed away. A blue wall rose behind Lobo, leaving only Vampie and the seven council members in the room with him.

"Prepare yourself, Lobo Coronado. You'll learn more about your family in the next few moments than you've known your entire life."

CHAPTER SIX:
A VISUAL BLOODLINE

Lobo put his hands in his pockets so no one could see his hands shaking.

"It was your grandfather who contacted you," Alina said. "After the deaths of your parents, he agreed that it would be best if we hid you. We kept you somewhere close to him, though, since he was your only living relative. Only two members of the council knew your whereabouts at first. A few years ago, your grandfather discovered your location and assigned Mr. Kindly to watch over you. What I don't understand is why he would send you here and not tell you all this himself."

"He said I would need to see for myself, then I would be able to trust him."

"He has a point. Knowing your grandfather, I wouldn't trust him if I had just met him, either." Alina leaned forward and turned toward the end of the council seats. "I ask you, Thornos, representative of the Tribe of Veyar, to approach our guest."

A creature with a scaly head rose from his seat and

walked toward the Earthling. Lobo noticed that the creature had large indentations on each side of his bald head that throbbed as he breathed.

Thornos stopped next to Lobo and then faced his peers. "I am pleased to serve the council, my Queen."

Alina rose. "Vonqua, stand next to Lobo."

Once he was in place, Alina stepped down from her throne and faced the three.

"Lobo, we are going to see moments of your past. Thornos is Veyaran, and his race has the ability to travel to any being's thread of history. With only a touch, he can travel to almost any past point in not only your life but also anyone of your bloodline."

"Bloodline? You mean my parents?" Lobo asked.

"Your parents and their parents, all the way back for generations. Know that you can only see the past. You won't be able to interact with anyone or anything. Are you prepared for this?"

Lobo stroked his medallion. "Yes."

Thornos faced Lobo. His temples started to glow.

"The time lobes within Thornos must be stimulated," Alina explained. "To do so, you must strike him. Firmly."

Thornos pointed to his temples, showing Lobo where to hit him.

Lobo reached his hand out and tapped the side of Thornos's head with a few fingers.

"My lobes are embedded deep within my temples, Lobo Coronado," Thornos said. "You must strike harder. I assure you, you won't hurt me. Strike me as hard as you can."

Lobo clenched his fist and smacked Thornos across the temple, making his head jerk to the side. Lobo winced from the pain as Thornos's lobes burned a bright blue. The light thickened and encompassed them all, then morphed into an electric tube that accelerated from within like a supersonic train.

"We are traveling in the memory lines of your family, Lobo," Alina said as sparks of electricity buzzed by her head. "Thornos, take us to his father's battle with Malong."

The tube train stopped. They were in the middle of a farm field on Earth and everything was still. A barn was in the background and a tractor stood nearby. Near the tractor, a muscular man in a grey leather coat was standing before a big creature with long claws extending from its hands. The man was holding a sword. Both were frozen as if a pause button had been pressed.

"Go," Alina said.

Everything started moving. The man and the creature known as Malong were in the middle of a fierce fight.

"That's my father," Lobo whispered.

"Sebastian Coronado," Alina began, "was an excellent detective, Lobo. This is his first encounter with a non-Earthbound being. Few Earthlings have ever seen a demon, but one of your father's cases led to this assassin being hired to kill him. Most men would have fled in fear, but your father chose to pull his favorite weapon, a Japanese katana sword, and fight without hesitation. He earned the title 'The Grey Wolf' by exhibiting this type of bravery as well as his crafty methods of solving cases."

Sebastian soon had Malong on his knees and then drove his sword through the creature's chest.

Alina continued. "Once we found out a human had destroyed a demon, we took notice. His investigations took him deeper into our world and eventually, we arranged a meeting with him. Thornos, please take us to his first council."

Another burst of light started the tube train again. They stopped and were back in the main council chamber.

Sebastian Coronado stood before the seated members. Lobo couldn't hear what the conversation was about but noticed his father kept shifting his gaze to a certain council member.

"Do you recognize the councilwoman who has piqued your father's interest?" Alina asked.

The woman seated the furthest to the right wore a hood that covered part of her face, but even under the cloak, her eyes sparkled. She pulled the hood back to speak, revealing golden hair that stretched down her back. Sebastian stopped talking and couldn't help but stare at the woman as her beauty radiated throughout the room.

"Mother," Lobo said. "That's my mother."

"Yes, Lobo. Your mother, Kira, was a member of this council. She was from the Tribe of Baia. As you can see, she and your father had a special connection the first time they met."

Lobo tried to speak but was only able to muster a grunt.

"Please take us to the wedding, Thornos," Alina said.

The tube train accelerated. Lobo felt the cracking electricity buzzing near his head, but his mind was racing and he paid it no notice.

They stopped in an open field with a large crowd of people. Lobo's mother and father were standing before the crowd. His mother was dressed in a long black and white gown decorated with bright gems. She looked as happy as his father, who was beaming, wearing a grey tuxedo with a long grey leather coat.

"Your mother resigned her council standing to be with your father. She gave up so much of her life to marry him. She could no longer return to any of the upper realms without being directly invited. Your father spent more time here than she did after they married."

"Why?"

"Your father worked with us. We are a peaceful realm and not permitted to interfere with violent Earth matters except for extreme, approved conditions. The Grey Wolf helped when we could not."

"Was my mother sad?" Lobo asked as his parents exchanged their wedding vows in the background.

Alina waved to Thornos and they moved again as Lobo stared at his feet.

"Look, Lobo," Alina whispered.

They were in his house. Mom was sitting in a rocking chair, holding a baby. She laughed as she tickled little Lobo's stomach with her nose and he broke into a hysterical cackle.

"She wasn't sad. She missed her world and her friends, but nothing could have made her happier than being with you." Alina put her hand on Lobo's shoulder. "It's time to go back."

"Can we please see more?" Lobo's voice cracked.

"No, Lobo. This is enough for now."

The tube lit up again and stopped back in the council chamber. Thornos rubbed his temples until his lobes stopped glowing.

Alina returned to her throne. "Lobo, I'm sure the little you have seen has led to more questions. Unfortunately, time is critical. I am going to ask you something that you may find surprising to ask of a young boy, but it needs your complete understanding."

Lobo nodded. "Okay."

"We are asking for you to help us find out who has started the Zaan," Alina said. "The Zaan is a series of events that lead to a ceremony meant to give one person on Earth enough power to either take it over or destroy it."

Lobo started to speak but stammered on his words.

"You want to ask how, which is understandable. If you

agree, you will return to Cornelius Coronado, the man who sent you here."

"My grandfather," Lobo said.

"He's your only known family on Earth and will guide you. Things will eventually become clearer, but it's important that you see him soon. Although I cannot go with you, I will send you some help. For now, you may ask me any questions, so long as it is not about your parents. I cannot give you any answers that will satisfy your thirst for more knowledge with the time we have. Your grandfather would probably be a better resource."

Lobo took a moment to gather his thoughts. "You said the Malong was from a demon realm. What does that mean?"

"There are six demon realms," Alina explained. "They are filled with animals and beings as diverse as what you've seen on Osidian, but they have demon blood running in their veins. A realm is another world, but not a planet such as Earth. It's just another place in time."

"So, is this a realm of heaven?"

"Not exactly. Osidian is the central world of the seven Celestial Tribes. Our closest ties to heaven are that our race of Cherubim are descendants of angels. Otherwise, we are similar to humans and have jobs and purpose."

"How come I don't remember having a grandfather, and why didn't he adopt me when my parents died?"

"Cornelius spent several years in our realms, gathering information to help your father, although he used a lot of that knowledge for his own personal gain. Other than your birth, I don't think he saw much of you."

Lobo shook his head. "Why me? I don't understand how I can help. I'm nobody."

"What makes you special, Lobo Coronado, is that not only was your father an extraordinary detective, but you have the blood of your mother running through you. If you exhibit any of their traits, it is worth pursuing."

Lobo still couldn't understand. "But I'm just a boy."

"Children have fought many great battles over the course of our history as well as Earth's. Your will and your heart, not your age, are what are important."

"What if I don't have any of their strengths?"

"All we are asking is that you take the first steps. We want to know if you inherited their abilities, and I would expect after all that you've learned today that you would be just as curious. You can refuse at any time. Even with your background, I do not think you should do this just because your father did."

"Then why?"

"This could give you a rare purpose in life. You would be opening yourself up to worlds that few people on Earth have ever seen. You would never be considered a nobody here."

Lobo's insides felt numb. "Okay, I'm willing to try. What do I have to do?"

"For now, go to your grandfather. I know this is overwhelming and I will not leave you to deal with this alone."

Alina extended her hand to Vampie. "Vonqua, Cornelius only gave me a moment's notice that Lobo was on his way and it was no coincidence that he appeared through the portal nearest you. I would like to request your help for our young friend."

Vampie was surprised. "Thank you for your confidence, Queen Alina, but how can I help?"

"How old are you now, Vonqua?" Alina asked.

"One thousand two hundred and seven years old."

"Of those years, how long have you trained for Scribeship?"

"The last four hundred."

"And you've worked in several different trades over the centuries, correct?"

"Yes. I've probably had more than a hundred different jobs. I've been a messenger, a driver of more types of vehicles than I can count and a researcher of different worlds, to name a few."

"I am offering you your first assignment as an official Scribe. Your wide range of knowledge, especially your research on Earth and its history, will be a great benefit to this assignment. Will you accept?"

Vampie bowed. "Thank you for the honor, Queen Alina. I do accept."

Lobo raised his hand, something the Academy had made him accustomed to when interrupting. "What do you mean by Vampie being a Scribe?"

"Vampie?" she asked, clearly amused by the nickname.

"It was easier for me to say," Lobo explained. "He seems to like it."

"We try to keep detailed records for historical purposes. A Scribe records all events that transpire."

"So, he'll be taking notes?"

"Yes, but a vampire may prove to be a useful companion outside of his Scribe duties. I still have another." Alina pressed something on her chair. "Bring her in."

Devon walked in with her Sprite escorts and tried swatting them away from her head. She looked down and didn't make eye contact with Alina. She took in a deep breath before speaking. "This wasn't my fault. Kai hurt Gira and I wanted to help, but he made me. . ."

"Devon," Alina interrupted. "That's not why you are here."

Devon's cheeks lightened. "Oh. Then disregard what I

just said about Kai."

"I'd like you to meet Lobo Coronado, Devon."

"Coronado?" Devon asked. "As in Sebastian?"

"Yes, this is his son."

Devon's eyebrows rose as she studied Lobo.

"I'm not sure if you're acquainted with Vonqua the Vampire," Alina said.

"I've seen him writing out in the pastures a few times."

"And I must confess," Vampie replied, "that I've heard your name before."

"Hmmph. Don't believe everything you hear, Vampire," Devon said.

Alina cleared her throat.

Devon crossed her arms. "Don't believe most things, I mean."

"It is a pleasure to formally meet you," Vampie said.

"Yeah," Devon replied. "Same here."

"Devon," Alina began, "I have offered a task to Lobo, which he has accepted. Vonqua is to be his Scribe."

Devon snickered. "A vampire Scribe? Does he write in blood?"

"No, Devon. This is an Earth task but affects us all. I have brought you here to ask for your assistance. I want you to go with them."

"Why would I want to do that? An Earth boy, a scribbling vampire and me. The Freaksome Threesome. I don't think so."

"It is your choice, young Cherubim. However, please clarify something for me. What is your goal in existence?"

Devon's forehead wrinkled. "To be chosen as a Guardian."

"A Guardian. The Cherubs that are called up are few. This could carry weight, giving you valuable experience, don't you think? It may even overshadow the many fights, threats and general mouth pollution that you tend to be so fond of."

Devon closed her eyes and nodded. "I'll go."

"Wonderful, Devon. I knew you would leap at the chance to help. Your only constraint is that you try to keep a low profile, so keep your wings covered. You will be leaving soon. Do you require anything?"

"I'm good."

"Vampire, do you need supplies?"

Vampie took a quick look into the pouch strapped across his back. "I have enough ink and parchment."

"Excuse me, Queen Alina," Lobo began. "Except for her wings, Devon could pass as human, but how will Vampie not get noticed?"

"That shouldn't be a problem, Lobo."

Lobo didn't ask for more details.

"Go directly to your grandfather, Cornelius," Alina instructed. "He will determine your place and the best course of action. You will return to the portal that brought you here. Mr. Kindly will be there."

"Okay," Lobo said.

"Devon, please join them," Alina requested.

Devon walked toward Lobo and Vampie. The top of her head barely reached Lobo's shoulder.

"Be safe," Alina said.

Alina waved her hand and two round, crystal objects appeared on either side of the group. Lights shot out of each object and connected, forming a large diamond around the three. The diamond filled with a bright light and they disappeared.

CHAPTER SEVEN:
THE FREAKSOME THREESOME

"How was your first trip to Osidian?" a familiar voice asked.

"It was nicer than this," Lobo replied, trying to catch his breath.

He, Devon and Vampie were scrunched together in the doghouse. Mr. Kindly and Killer B were looking in.

"They look like three pieces of chewed gum stuck under a chair, don't they B?" Mr. Kindly asked his dog.

Killer B barked in agreement.

"Vampie," Lobo said. "Do you think you can squeeze out?"

Devon's foot went into Lobo's mouth and stopped him in mid-sentence, making him gag.

"Can you move your foot?"

"I would if I could."

Vampie, who was smaller and more flexible, squirmed his way out of the doghouse. He left enough space for Devon and Lobo to follow.

Lobo introduced Vampie and Devon to Mr. Kindly.

Vampie complimented him on the gardens, then walked toward one with bright red flowers.

"Are those Boowallas?"

"Yes, one of my favorites."

"You have flowers from Osidian here?" Vampie asked. "That has to violate a few laws. Their pollen could carry disease."

Mr. Kindly stuck his nose against Vampie's. "There's no violation if no one opens their mouth, is there?"

Vampie stepped back. "I suppose not. Nice gardens."

Killer B was growling and Devon was staring him down.

Mr. Kindly got between them. "Leave my dog alone, Cherub."

"If he drools on my foot again, I'll shove him under one of your daisies."

"There's no time to waste. Lobo's grandfather sent a car," Mr. Kindly explained. "Apparently, my job has shifted from observer to driver."

He led them to the front of his house. He took a careful look around, but no one was nearby. He rushed them to the waiting black stretch limousine, held the door open for the trio and they hurried inside.

"Watch the house and my gardens," Mr. Kindly yelled at Killer B before getting in the driver's seat.

Kindly raised the glass divider between the front and back seats No one said much the first few moments of the ride. Devon stared at her feet. Lobo tried to process all that had happened and Vampie's Finger Quills were flying, describing the limousine and the surroundings he observed through the window. Devon mumbled something, which broke Lobo's trance.

"Devon," Lobo asked. "What did Alina mean about becoming a Guardian and you being an angel descendant?"

Devon blew her hair out of her face. "The Cherubim are a class of angels in heaven and our race on Osidian is a distant bloodline. The true angels run the show, but we help with some of the guardian work."

"You mean for humans?" Lobo asked.

"There are many worlds that can have Guardians, but I hope to be assigned to Earth."

"Why Earth?"

"I've always been fascinated with humans. I thought it would be interesting."

"So, does this mean we all have our own guardian angel?" Lobo asked.

"Not necessarily. Guardians help people as a whole and are usually only assigned to a single person for a short time, but there are special situations where it may last longer."

Lobo gazed at Devon for a few minutes and noticed she hadn't looked up.

"Is this the first time you've been to Earth?"

"Yes, I've seen it in images and once through a viewing crystal, even though I was kind of looking over someone's shoulder at the time."

Lobo was confused. "What I don't get is if you've never been here, why don't you look excited?"

"I just don't like being forced to do anything," Devon explained. "I wanted to come here on my own terms."

"How long do you have to wait to become a Guardian?"

"It can take one year or hundreds of years. I'm only twenty, but far from adulthood in my world. To be considered, you must set a good example of wanting to help others and try to be as pure as possible. My temper sometimes gets in the way."

"So, why send you with us?"

"I don't know. It's a test, I guess."

Vampie stopped writing. "And maybe for your

abilities?"

Devon shrugged. "I suppose that makes more sense."

"What abilities?" Lobo asked.

"Since the Cherubim have angel blood," Devon explained, "we have some divine power. We can do some basic enchantments, manipulate objects and perform transformations. There are others, some that are unique to each Cherub."

Devon turned to Vampie. "Speaking of transformations, what are we going to do about your appearance, Vampire?"

"What's wrong with my appearance?"

"I don't think you can go unnoticed here. There aren't many creatures that you could pass for."

"What about your wings, Devon?" Lobo asked.

Devon flashed a crooked smile, closed her eyes and held her hands out, palms up. Her wings glowed and shrunk until they were unnoticeable. "There, now I look like a young Earth girl."

"Cool," Lobo said. "What about Vampie?"

"Vampie? I guess that sounds better than Vonqua. Vampires can transform into different animals. Show him, Vampie."

Vampie stood on the seat and shifted into a six-winged dragon with one eye. He then switched to an odd shaped rat with a duck's bill.

Lobo shook his head. "Those won't work. Can you become an Earth creature?"

"I'm not sure. These are animals I've tried to emulate my entire life. It's not easy to do new ones."

Devon cracked her knuckles. "I may be able to help you with that, Vampire."

"He did think I was a dog when he first saw me," Lobo said. "Then he barked like one to try and communicate."

Devon crossed her arms. "A dog? That could work. You don't have any fur, though."

Lobo rubbed his temples. "What about a Chihuahua? They're hairless. Do you know what they look like?"

Devon rubbed a finger down Vampie's nose. "I think so." She touched Vampie's head. His eyes grew large, but he didn't protest. An instant later, his pointy ears shrunk, his body twisted and his nose extended into a snout.

Vampie stood on all fours. "How's this?"

"Not bad," Lobo said, "but you still need a tail."

Devon slapped Vampie's rear and a thin tail appeared.

Lobo clapped his hands. "You're a little big for a Chihuahua, but I'll tell people you're a mixed breed."

"What about my bag?"

Devon wrapped the bag around the vampire. Its material conformed to his dog shape. "Now it looks like a sweater."

"You're not going to make me chase any balls, are you?" Vampie asked.

Lobo smiled. "No. You just have to get me the paper every morning."

"If you need to switch forms, just say. . ." Devon tapped her lower lip, deep in thought. "Just say 'Hail Queen Devon.'"

Vampie smirked. "I'm sure your modesty will help you up the Guardian career ladder."

The car stopped.

"Looks like it's time to get out," Lobo said. "I don't see anyone, so I think it's safe."

Vampie mumbled, "Hail Queen Devon," and changed back to himself as Mr. Kindly opened the door.

They were parked in front of a building that looked like a warehouse. There were seven portable storage rooms next to it. There were no paved parking lots, just a dirty and dusty ground. Kindly pointed to the building door.

"Do we just walk in?" Lobo asked.

Kindly didn't answer, but continued to point. Lobo paused, then headed to the building.

Devon stared down Kindly. "You have some kind of communication problem all of a sudden?"

Mr. Kindly didn't react. "Just doing as I'm told."

Vampie nudged Devon and they followed Lobo.

They entered the unlocked doors and went into a big open space filled with a mess of wood, broken glass, nails and sawdust.

"Hello?" Lobo called out.

A voice cracked over a speaker that none of them could see. "Step toward the broken doors."

Lobo scanned the room and saw two mangled doors that formed a small pyramid. He stepped over the debris, avoiding the glass shards and jagged wood until he was in front of the doors. Devon and Vampie mimicked his steps. There was a loud crack and the doors separated. The pyramid slid apart, revealing a stairway underneath.

Lobo paused and looked at his companions. "What do I do?"

"You have to take the first step sometime," Devon said as she started down the stairs.

Lobo let out a big breath. "Okay, then." He and Vampie followed.

The stairwell was dark at first, but a dim blue light turned on as the doors above closed. After a few hundred feet of winding stairs, they reached another door and walked through.

The room they entered was half the size of a football field. There were more doors in the back and the walls held various weapons.

A statue of an eight-foot black blob stood at the end of

the room.

A familiar sound echoed in the room. One of the back doors opened and Lobo's grandfather, Cornelius Coronado, entered.

"You saw Alina?" Cornelius asked.

"Yes."

"Did she confirm what I told you?"

Lobo nodded.

"Did you accept the task?"

"I did."

"Can you tell me why?"

Lobo was surprised by the question. "I'm not sure."

"You must have had a reason. Could it be because you thought it was what your father would have done?"

Lobo looked down and rubbed one of his shoes with the other. "Maybe."

Cornelius's mechanical body hovered closer. Lobo saw him take a quick look at his companions as Vampie wrote in his notebook.

"A vampire Scribe? Interesting. Your father never allowed a Scribe to accompany him. He worked alone. What about the Cherub?"

"The Scribe's name is Vampie, and her name is Devon. She's here to help me," Lobo answered.

"A cousin to the angels sent here. I am not foolish enough to question Alina's reasoning. She did contact me before your arrival but said nothing of your companions. She took the news of me finding you rather well. That means that she knows we need you."

"Alina said I was hidden from you, but you found out where I was a long time ago. Why did you wait so long to come get me?"

"I didn't want to endanger you, which is why I had no intention of reaching out until you were older. However, a little more than a year ago, I found a link among several missing Earth artifacts that pointed toward the possibility of the Zaan. I know you are only thirteen and it was only after careful consideration that I thought you might be able to help."

"I'm almost fourteen. So you only contacted me because you needed me."

"Being needed isn't such a terrible thing, Jeremiah. We'll start slow. For your first mission, I only want you to observe."

"He's just a boy," Devon said.

"The son of a Coronado that is half Baian could be much more than an ordinary boy. Lobo, step forward onto the center seal."

Lobo moved toward the middle of the room. A grey wolf seal was painted into the center of the floor. He stood right on it.

Lobo was staring at the seal when he heard a fast whooshing sound and realized something was flying at his head. Without thinking, he shifted his body to one side and clasped his hands together, catching the object. Devon jumped toward Lobo, but couldn't have reached him in time.

"What are you doing?" Devon yelled.

Lobo looked at the object in his hands and saw a glistening dagger. Its blade was five inches long and its handle was made of bone. The bottom of the handle bore the face of a dragon with its tongue sticking out.

"How?" Lobo couldn't complete his sentence.

Devon grabbed a spear off the wall and rushed to Cornelius. An electric charge shot out of the hover chair and knocked the Cherub back.

"I had to know, Lobo. Your father had many natural abilities. He was quick and had almost a sixth sense when it came to danger. He was also able to master many weapons in a short time. I suspected you had similar abilities. There's no doubt you're quick on your reaction time."

"What if I hadn't caught it?"

"The handle would have struck your head instead of the blade," Cornelius explained.

Lobo was too surprised to be angry.

Devon regained her senses and was preparing to attack again.

Lobo raised his hand. "It's okay, Devon."

"You're not the one that just got zapped," Devon snapped.

"Yeah, I was just almost stabbed in the head."

Devon eased back. "Okay, you win."

"Lobo, in your years at the Academy," Cornelius began, "were you ever in a situation where you noticed you were faster than the other boys?"

Lobo thought as he felt the handle of the dagger.

"I only got into one real fight. The two biggest kids at the Academy, Oscar and Jerry, attacked my friend Kyle. I tried to jump in and Oscar threw a big rock at the back of my head. Without thinking, just like now, I caught the rock without looking and threw it back. I cut his eye open."

"Good. He got what he deserved," Devon chimed in.

Lobo continued. "After I hit Oscar, Jerry came after me, but he couldn't touch me after swinging four or five times. He finally fell over and a bunch of kids jumped on him and started punching. Both of them cried in front of everybody. They never messed with us again after that."

"Even with your natural speed and reaction time, you still need training," Cornelius said.

Devon stepped forward but kept her distance. "I thought this was just going to be a mission to observe."

"Yes, but you must always be prepared. What if you're caught?"

"Why can't your people go out on this mission, then?" the Cherub protested. "Wouldn't they be ready?"

"We've already found evidence of demons guarding locations we're monitoring on Earth. The person responsible could be a demon himself. Every time my people have gotten close to suspicious activity, the suspects disappear. They must be caught off guard, and the last thing they would expect are children."

"When do we start?" Lobo asked.

"You will begin preparing tomorrow. I have several hotspots I'd like to have checked again. We need to find out if any of them hold information on the Zaan. However, you will need to undergo stealth training first."

Vampie raised his quills. "What is stealth?"

"Stealth is the ability to sneak around without anyone seeing you," Cornelius answered. "You will also be taught different combat and weapon techniques."

"I'm ready," Lobo said. "Let's start now."

"You have had enough for the day. You've adapted well to all that's been shown to you, but I want you to take one night to process it and get some rest. It's important that you have your head together before we start the training program. For tonight, you will need to stay with Mr. Kindly."

"Why would I do that? Can't we just stay here?"

"The Academy has kept you safe and Mr. Kindly has been able to keep watch over you all this time without incident. However, if I was able to find you, someone else could do the same. I think Mr. Kindly is the better option. I have given him instructions on what to do. I will send for you tomorrow. Now go."

CHAPTER EIGHT: AMIGOS

When they returned to the car they were greeted by a different driver. He was stocky and didn't speak, and was built like a linebacker.

"Where's Mr. Kindly?" Lobo asked, but the driver didn't respond.

It was past ten o'clock when they arrived at Mr. Kindly's house. The driver got out and held the car door open. Mr. Kindly waited at the door. The three entered and were taken aback when they first saw him. His hair was short and neat and he wore a suit and round glasses that made him look like a college professor.

Before Lobo could ask, Mr. Kindly started to speak. "I am going to speak with your headmaster. We need a plan to make the Cherub and the vampire look presentable in case we have unexpected company."

"We're way ahead of you on that one," Lobo said as he motioned toward Vampie.

"Hail Queen Devon," Vampie said as he transformed into a Chihuahua.

"Not bad. Devon, I've brought you some clothes."

Mr. Kindly handed Devon a bag. She unzipped it, waved her hand and her clothes were replaced with jeans and a tee-shirt. Her hair shortened. It was still long and uncombed, but she looked like a normal Earth girl.

"Good, good. Now I'm going to be your long lost uncle on your mother's side." Mr. Kindly instructed.

"What's your name going to be?" Lobo asked.

Mr. Kindly's eyes got big as he panicked. He hadn't thought that far ahead. "I don't know. A flower's name is fine."

"Uncle Daisy?" Vampie asked.

Mr. Kindly slapped his hand against the front door. "That's a girl's name. How about Uncle Bud?"

"Uncle Butt?" Devon asked.

"Bud! With a 'd'."

"Ohhh," Devon and Vampie said.

"Devon, you are his cousin. Since Devon can be a girl or boy's name on Earth, you can keep it. Same goes for you, vampire. Vampie's a weird dog name, but it'll do. Everyone straight?"

The three nodded.

"I brought you some extra clothes as well, Lobo. They're in the same bag."

Lobo unzipped the bag and rifled through it. There were a few pairs of blue jeans and several dark, long-sleeved tees.

"How did you know this is what I usually wear?"

"I've watched you long enough to know your poor taste in clothing. Now don't leave the house. I'll be back as soon as I can. There's food on the table."

Kindly closed the door behind him and walked into the waiting car.

Lobo hadn't realized how hungry he was until Kindly

mentioned food.

The three turned. They had been standing in a foyer and walked into a nice living room. There was a long couch facing a big screen television mounted on the wall. An oversized green recliner was in the back of the room. The only items on the walls were a few pictures of Killer B. Lobo glanced at them but kept following the smell of food.

They passed into the dining room, where a long cherry wood table was covered with steaming plates. One plate was filled with turkey slices and another with roast beef. A third had pizza slices and the rest were stacked with fruit, cakes and cookies. Mr. Kindly was definitely prepared.

Lobo wanted to grab handfuls of food and shove them in his mouth but thought he might set a bad example for his companions. He sat down and used his fork to grab each piece of meat. Devon and Vampie studied each food item before eating it but enjoyed every bite. They didn't say a word as they filled their stomachs.

Lobo and Devon were on their second helping of chocolate cake, but Vampie liked the cookies. He was on his tenth one when Killer B started barking.

The three rushed back to the living room and looked out the window. B was at the fence, barking nonstop.

"Lobo, are you there?" a tiny voice yelped.

"It's Kyle!" Lobo said, opening the door.

"Keep him quiet," Devon snapped. "We're supposed to be hidden."

Lobo rushed out the door. Killer B turned to face him. Lobo took slow steps as he neared the dog. "Good Killer B. Don't eat my friend, please."

Killer B lowered his head and sat on his front legs.

Lobo opened the fence door.

"Come inside," Lobo said.

Kyle didn't take his eyes off B and rushed up the

walkway and through the front door with Lobo right behind.

"Kindly," Kyle was trying to catch his breath. "I heard him tell the headmaster you were here and that he was your uncle. Is this true?"

"Sit down, Kyle," Lobo said, motioning toward the living room couch.

"I thought you ran away, Lobo," Kyle said.

"You know I wouldn't leave without telling you goodbye or taking you with me."

Kyle looked relieved and stuck his palm out. "Still amigos?"

Lobo slapped Kyle's hand. "Amigos forever."

Devon's forehead wrinkled. "What's an omeego?"

"It's 'amigo,' Devon, and it means friend. Kyle is my best friend."

Kyle stared at Devon. "Is this your cousin that Kindly was talking about?"

"Not exactly. There's something I have to tell you, Kyle."

Devon nudged Lobo with her elbow and Vampie, who was back to his dog form, yelped.

"Kyle's the only family I've had these last few years. He's the closest thing I have to a real brother. If I can't trust him, I can't trust anyone."

Vampie growled, but Devon flicked his nose with her finger and then turned to Lobo. "We understand, Lobo. Go ahead."

Lobo stood in front of his friend and raised his little finger. "This is big, Kyle. I need you to pinkie handshake swear that this stays with us."

Kyle extended his hand and they locked pinkie fingers, then lifted their hands and snapped their wrists down like a whip. They then broke into an elaborate exchange that ended with them spinning their hands and knocking their knuckles twice.

Vampie jumped and tried to pull a quill from his bag, but he couldn't get the bag open with his little paws.

"Kyle, before I start the story, you need to know about Devon and the Chihuahua. Devon's not exactly human. She's. . ." Lobo paused for a moment. "She's kind of like an almost-angel."

Devon's curly hair returned and she extended her small wings. Kyle's eyes widened, but he didn't say a word.

"Don't yell or freak," Lobo continued. "Just trust me. The Chihuahua isn't really a dog, either. He's a vampire."

Vampie smiled, revealing his sharp fangs.

Kyle's face turned red and he put his hand around his neck to protect it.

"He's not like the vampires we've seen in the movies," Lobo explained.

"Does he drink blood?" Kyle asked, struggling to get the words out.

"Yes, but not human blood. Only animals, but he doesn't kill them. He's not scary looking, either."

Lobo nodded to Vampie.

"Hail Queen Devon," Vampie whispered.

Kyle still backed away as Vampie transformed. Vampie snatched his quill and started writing.

"He's harmless, Kyle. His job is to write down everything that's happening."

Vampie finished scribbling and reached his hand out. "Good to meet you."

Kyle took Vampie's hand and shook it. His body eased.

"Are you ready for the rest?" Lobo asked.

Kyle's mouth stayed open as Lobo explained all that had happened over the last day.

Once Lobo was done with his tale, Kyle took a big

breath. "Wow, so what happens now?"

Devon jumped in front of Kyle. "You believe everything, just like that?"

Kyle nodded. "Like Lobo said, if we can't trust each other, we can't trust anyone. Plus, your wings and his fangs were pretty convincing."

"I think we'll be gone during most of the next few days," Lobo said. "But we should be back at night to sleep here. Just tell anyone who asks that I'm spending time with my long-lost uncle."

"I will."

"What is that?" Devon asked, pointing to a chain dangling from Kyle's hand.

Kyle stared at his fist and pulled out a necklace with a locket on it. He opened the locket, revealing the picture of a woman.

"Isn't that. . ." Devon began.

"It's Lobo's mom," Kyle said. "I never knew my parents, so Lobo told me I could pretend she was my mom, too. I talk to her sometimes. It makes me feel better."

"Amigos, right?" the Cherub said. "You may not carry the same blood, but you are true brothers."

CHAPTER NINE:
VIRTUAL FIGHTER

Mr. Kindly returned an hour later and Kyle snuck out the back door before he walked in. He set up the trio in one bedroom. Lobo and Devon had their own beds, but Vampie slept as a Chihuahua on a padded chair.

Kindly woke them up early the next morning and fed them a full breakfast of bacon, eggs and toast. He returned them to the warehouse to meet Cornelius in the training room.

Cornelius hovered by the large blob statue and didn't dispense any greetings when the Freaksome Threesome arrived.

"Stealth can be more useful than fighting," the old man said. "If you're not seen, you won't have to fight. It may not be the most glamorous skill you want to learn, but it is the most important. The Gornda here will help with most of your training."

The blob statue moved. It oozed off its base and separated into four pieces. Each piece rose and formed into neckless creatures with metal rings pierced through their shoulders.

"The Gornda can shape into almost any form. These round beasts are Korindian guards. They have a sense of smell and detection that are only bested by bloodhounds. Their weaknesses are that they're slow and they have poor eyesight. These are what we will have to get around first."

"How do you know?" Lobo asked.

"I told you we've found evidence of demons on Earth. We've discovered traces of these guards in three different places, and think that one of those locations holds the person in charge. Now, let's start by creating a setting for you to practice."

Cornelius hit some buttons on his chair. Walls of light started rising from the floor. One wall went straight through Lobo and made him jump.

"It's a hologram, Jeremiah," Cornelius explained. "It won't hurt any of you. Not yet, at least."

The walls rose and then solidified, leaving the trio standing in an alley. One end led to a well-lit street and the other led to a darker, dirtier area with ladders and doors every few yards.

Although they could no longer see him, Cornelius's voice echoed from above. "Everything around you will feel solid and real now. You need to get deeper into the alley without looking guilty. Just try to act normal."

A Korindian came out of the darkness. Devon flattened herself against a wall and Vampie cowered in a corner. Lobo stood out in the open and froze. The guard rushed toward them and then drew a sword with a fat blade. He made a striking motion straight at Lobo's head. As the sword hit Lobo, a shock ran through his body and he fell.

"Dead," the guard's low voice boomed.

"You didn't look like innocent children playing with their dog," Cornelius said.

"I thought they couldn't hurt us!" Lobo yelled.

"The room's floor allows me to send electric voltage wherever I want. Helps simulate being attacked. Had that been real, I am certain you would have been in much more pain. Now, try again."

The guard disappeared.

Lobo looked at Devon, who didn't offer any help. He checked back toward the street and saw a basketball at the brighter end of the alley. He walked over and picked it up, then turned and threw the ball over Devon's head. "Catch!"

Devon was caught off guard but still tried to reach for the ball as it flew past her and landed near some doors. Lobo ran to the ball with Devon and Vampie following.

"Do you hear that?" Devon asked.

Lobo stuck his ear up to a door. "There's something banging around in there."

"Better," Cornelius said. "Follow your instincts."

Lobo reached for the door, but it was locked. He checked the ground and found a nail. He stuck it in the keyhole and jiggled it.

"Are you a master locksmith that can pick any lock?" Cornelius asked.

"No."

"Then why make noise and bring attention to yourself when you know you can't open the door?"

"What am I supposed to do then?"

Devon pulled his hand back and touched the lock. Her wings rose underneath her shirt and emitted a soft glow through the cloth as the lock clicked open.

"You could've just asked," Devon said.

"I didn't know you could. . ."

"You see why the Cherub is here, Jeremiah," Cornelius said. "Be mindful of your surroundings, Devon. There are demons that can detect celestial magic from short range."

They entered the door. Vampie and Lobo rushed inside.

"The dead can hear your footsteps," Cornelius said. "Move slowly and step softly."

Vampie and Lobo stopped cold. Lobo took his next step in slow motion.

Devon dashed by them. Her footsteps didn't make a sound as she reached a long staircase ahead.

"Devon," Lobo said in a loud whisper. "Wait for us."

Devon folded her arms as Lobo and Vampie caught up. The stairs led up to a platform that turned left and right and formed a big square walkway. As they neared the last few steps before the platform, Lobo noticed a guard approaching from one of the far ends.

"Get down," Lobo warned.

"He's going to see us," Devon said.

"Cornelius said they have bad eyesight. Let's crawl the other way," Lobo said.

Lobo crawled up the last few stairs and onto the platform. He headed in the opposite direction of the guard as Devon and Vampie followed. The guard hadn't seen them yet, but the gap between them was closing.

Lobo nudged Devon and pointed to a stack of crates. He crawled faster and soon all three of them were behind the crates. They stuck their heads up and saw the guard turn around.

"We're safe," Lobo said. "I guess we're quick learners."

"Dead," a loud voice snarled behind them. The trio turned as a second guard slashed its sword through all three of them in one stroke. The shock knocked Vampie back into a stack of crates that crashed down on him.

"My apologies, Vampire. The shock was too strong for your body size," Cornelius said. "Much better, all of you. Always check every direction, even when you think the danger has passed. You'll probably run into more than one guard at a time."

"When do you teach him to fight?" Devon asked. "In case he does get caught?"

"First, the stealth. Survive a simulation mission for more than five minutes before you start worrying about combat. Start again."

They continued stealth training late into the evening, stopping only for a few minutes to eat.

They were killed many times, but Vampie took the record for the day, taking more than fifty zaps.

They returned to Kindly's house exhausted. The next few days were about the same. They trained only on stealth and by the third day, they were able to get around more than thirty guards. Even Vampie had improved, taking only two or three shocks on the last few runs.

On the fifth day of training, the three arrived to find the Gornda broken into ten blob pieces standing around the training floor.

"Jeremiah," Cornelius began. "I didn't want to start this until at least a few more days, but time is against us. No more stealth. Today, we fight."

Devon grinned. "It's about time."

"Did something happen?" Lobo asked.

"We have noticed an increase in activity and may need to move soon. I need to prepare you to defend yourself."

"Let's do it," Lobo said.

The blobs changed. Half of them turned into Korindians, but the others took on the shape of a different creature. They had bony bodies, thick necks and heads like a ram, only with thinner horns. They also bared sharp teeth.

"These are Barna, Jeremiah. They are lower level, unintelligent demons, but are fast and can injure with their claws and teeth. If you get past the Korindians, the Barna will be the next enemy sent to stop you."

"How do I fight them?" Lobo asked.

"For now, you just need to try and avoid them. Use your speed and adjust to their attacks. Devon, as a Cherub, I would expect you are able to use your angel abilities during a fight, correct?"

"Yes," Devon answered. "But I don't mind using my fists."

"I need to concentrate on Jeremiah. Take a Gornda into the smaller training room in the back, and have it form any enemy you'd like to fight."

Devon nodded and rushed after one of the Gornda.

"Vampire, you should not need to fight. The enemy will figure out you're a Scribe at some point. Even the vilest creatures in hell like to have their stories told, so I expect you will be safe."

Vampie let out a sigh of relief as he prepared a fresh parchment.

"Let's not waste any more time," Cornelius said as he glided out of the way.

A Korindian approached Lobo first. It lunged forward and swung its sword, but Lobo was able to step aside without much effort. The guard attacked a few more times, but never touched him.

"Excellent, Jeremiah. Your natural speed and instincts make it easy to avoid these hulking guards. The Barna, though, are a different story. Be ready."

The Guard returned to the outer ring of the room. The Barna stepped forward but then stood still. Lobo heard it breathing as it cracked its neck and spit dripped out of its mouth. It stared at Lobo, then snapped its claws and leapt hard at its target.

Lobo moved fast, but a claw scraped his face and a

sharp electric shot burned across his cheek. As he reached for his wound, he sensed the Barna rushing at him from behind. He ducked without thinking and the Barna flew over him. It landed on its bony knees but spun around for another attack. It leapt high in the air and landed in front of Lobo with its arm cocked back, ready to strike. Lobo dove to one side and the Barna missed. It punched three more times, but couldn't make contact.

Four more Barna joined in. Lobo twisted and turned to avoid the first three, but the fourth hit him in the chest.

Lobo yelled as he fell to the ground. The next Barna was already preparing to jump.

"Forget the pain and keep moving, Jeremiah," Cornelius instructed. "You might survive a scratch, but a few deep cuts from those claws and it's over."

Lobo rolled over and jumped back to his feet. The virtual demons continued their attack, but couldn't score another direct hit.

The Barna surrounded him and formed a circle. They lunged and Lobo panicked. All five hit him with electric strikes to the head and chest, knocking him back on the ground.

"You're thinking too much," Cornelius said. "Did you know what you were going to do when they attacked you one at a time?"

"No. I didn't have time to think."

"When they took their time and surrounded you, you started planning your next move, but you didn't have one. Trust your instincts. We'll start adding some offensive moves soon, but for now, try just avoiding them once more."

The Barna took their positions, surrounding Lobo again. This time, he took a moment to calm down. The Barna attacked. Lobo sensed them as they moved closer.

He twisted out of each attack and two of the Barna crashed into each other.

Cornelius nodded. "That was better, Jeremiah. Much better. You may be what we all were hoping for after all."

CHAPTER TEN: THE CALL

Mr. Kindly banged on the bedroom door before dawn the next morning. Devon jumped on her bed into a fighting stance. Vampie the Chihuahua fell out of the chair he was sleeping on, but Lobo kept snoring.

Devon slapped Lobo on the shoulder as Kindly entered the room.

"We have to go, Lobo," Mr. Kindly said. "Long day ahead."

Cornelius was waiting in the training room when they arrived. "Your performance over the last week has gone beyond my highest expectations. Your speed and even basic defensive moves would take most people months, even years, to learn. You definitely inherited some of Sebastian's skills. Today, we will add weapons to the mix."

A rack of staffs, swords and various other weapons stood to one side of the room. Devon and Lobo looked them over.

Vampie lifted a wooden three-pointed sai, then smacked himself on the nose after trying to flip it. "That one's dangerous."

Devon took the sai and flipped it over her head, then reached behind her back and caught it.

Lobo reached for the rack, then hesitated. "Cornelius, why not just use a gun?"

"Bullets are an easy weapon to deflect with magic and they are useless against demons. In most battles, you will be close enough to your enemy to see him sweat. You would be better off with a twig than a gun. Now, Jeremiah, it's time to choose a weapon."

Lobo remembered seeing his father fight the Malong and pulled out a long sword with a curved blade.

A Korindian guard appeared on the training floor.

Lobo slapped the blade against his hand. "This should be easy. They couldn't get near me yesterday, and now I have a sword."

The guard rushed and Lobo swung the sword, completely missing his target. The guard smacked Lobo's head from behind as he struggled to pick the heavy weapon back up.

"That's probably too bulky, Lobo," Devon said. "It takes away your speed advantage."

Cornelius agreed. "My sentiments exactly, Junior Angel."

Lobo put the sword back and extracted a shiny staff. It had a soft grip in the center and the ends had a slight curve. He spun it a few times.

"This feels good, but it's so light. I don't think it's strong enough."

"That is a staff made of metal cristalinium, which I'm sure you saw forms of on Osidian," Cornelius explained. "In its metallic form, cristalinium is stronger than titanium but as light as aluminum. It should complement your speed if you can get a feel for it."

Another Korindian approached. Lobo moved as smooth as the day before and spun his staff sideways, striking the guard across its chest. Lobo pulled the staff back and hit the guard on the head with the other end. A second guard appeared and Lobo grabbed the center grip with both hands. He struck both enemies within seconds of each other without much effort.

"Keep going," Cornelius said.

Three Barna moved in. Lobo was struck a few times but held his ground. He knocked a Barna down and was attempting a second strike at it when two others hit him from behind.

A loud wind resonated in the room as a Shadow Guard rushed toward Cornelius and whispered in his ear.

Cornelius fixated on his chair's view screen and hit several buttons.

"Jeremiah, training is over. You have to go into the field now."

The Korindians and Barna melted into black goo and slimed into each other, forming one large mass on the training floor that looked like an oil spill. The liquid then slid to its stand and took its original blob shape.

Lobo ran to his grandfather. "Is something wrong, Cornelius?"

"Activity has spiked beyond the highest levels we've seen. Something big is happening or is about to happen. Of the three hotspots we've been monitoring, one seems to have been abandoned while the other two are showing ten times their normal activity. Are you ready?"

Lobo nodded. "I think so."

"That weapon seems to have complemented you well. Press the small button by the handle."

Lobo found a small indention by the side of the handle and pressed it. The staff clicked and shrunk to the size of a pen.

"Only take one weapon so you don't waste time trying to decide which one to use. I will supply you with everything else. Follow me."

Lobo put the staff in his back pocket. The trio followed Cornelius and entered the back doorway, which led to a long hallway filled with several smoked glass doors. Cornelius stopped in front of a green door, hit a button and it slid open.

"Baron, are you here?" Cornelius shouted as he entered the room with Lobo and company right behind.

The room was filled with long tables that each held electronic pieces and metals of all shapes and sizes. It looked like an electronic junkyard. Something fell in the back of the room and a creature with long, thin arms emerged. Its arms moved sideways and flowed with each step as if they were painting the ground with long brushes. The creature didn't have any feet. Instead, it had a reptilian body that slithered like a snake. It had skin from the neck up that was a pale red color. It had two bulging eyes with red pupils and a small nose that looked human. One eye stared at Cornelius while the other moved up and down, studying the visitors.

"I am here, Cornelius. How may I be of service?"

Devon gasped. "Isn't that a Mogus?"

"Yes, Baron is a Mogus," Cornelius answered.

Lobo was lost. "What's that?"

"A demon," Devon said. "Your grandfather has a demon in his employment and I'd like to know why."

"True, Baron is a demon, and yes, he works for me. He built my chair and is the most brilliant engineer I have ever known. I enticed him from his demon realm."

"Why would it leave its realm?" Devon asked.

Baron grunted. "Cornelius offers much better benefits,

I assure you."

Cornelius' mechanical hand slapped against a table. "Enough. No one here has the right to question my choices of staff. Jeremiah, come here."

Lobo moved between Baron and his grandfather.

"Baron, I need a camera attached to the youngest living Coronado."

"Yesss sir," Baron hissed. He slid to a table filled with more junk. He hit a button and the metal pieces disappeared, leaving a shiny surface devoid of any mess. Baron moved toward some shelves and grabbed a few items before returning.

The demon reached out his bony fingers. "Give me your hand, Lobo Coronado."

Lobo hesitated.

"It's okay, Jeremiah," Cornelius said. "I trust Baron with my life."

Lobo put his hand on the table.

Baron grabbed Lobo's wrist and flipped his palm face up, then poked the boy's hand until he found the meatiest part of his flesh. "I am going to put a camera that will embed into the top layer of your skin right here. Tap it twice to toggle it on and off. It will dissolve after a few days and you won't even know it was there."

Lobo pulled his hand back. "Will it hurt?"

"Humans and their fear of pain. No, you'll just feel tingling as it breaks through."

Baron pulled out a shimmering orange object that was about the size of a dime. He laid it in the center of Lobo's palm. It brightened and seemed to burn through the boy's skin.

Lobo flexed his fingers. "That's not so. . ."

Large sparks popped and flew from Lobo's hand and hit a group of jars across the room. The pain stung, but

Lobo stayed calm.

"Unusual," Baron said as he inspected the palm. "That's never happened before."

Baron grabbed a small device that looked like a man's electric shaver. He ran it across Lobo's hand. "Everything's normal."

"They'll need communicators and a basic collapsing bag kit," Cornelius instructed.

Baron pulled out three small devices that looked like mechanical snails. "These will wriggle just inside your ear tunnel and take its shape."

Lobo took one and held it. Baron pulled out a thin prod and touched the snail, causing its shell to light up. Four legs snapped out of the object, and unlike a normal snail, it dashed up Lobo's arm and planted its legs just around his ear. Lobo was afraid to move. The snail turned into white slime, dripped into his ear and unwrapped itself inside until it filled the entire canal. Lobo grimaced, then keeled over and grabbed the side of his head.

Devon jumped. "Lobo, what's wrong? Are you okay?"

"Yes," he replied, holding his breath. "It just tickles like you wouldn't believe."

Devon and Vampie exhaled and grabbed their own snails. Within a few seconds, their communicators were also in place.

"The communicators are voice activated, so just say 'on' or 'off' to establish or break the connection," Baron said. "Now, your survival packs." He handed them each a black pouch. "This holds money, snacks, tools, navigation glasses and several other items you may need. You'll also be supplied with small cameras that will stick to almost anything. The pouch is the size of a quarter and will expand when you need to pull something out. It will feel empty, but just state what you want. Say 'money' if you want money."

Vampie tapped his quills. "Can I keep my parchment and writing supplies in it?"

"Yessss, Vampire. You can put your entire bag inside if you choose."

"Thank you, Baron," Cornelius said. "We may be coming back to you soon."

"What?" Baron said, surprised. "No fingerflames or wristknives?"

"Not yet, but maybe next time."

Baron's scaly body drooped. "A genius's work is never complete until his creations are truly appreciated."

"It's time to leave," Cornelius said.

Lobo threw his staff in the pouch and then stuffed it in his pocket. He felt the pouch shrink in his hands. "Where are we going?"

"The two locations are far apart. The first is in San Francisco and the other is in North Texas. We'll try San Francisco first. It's on the coast, so access is easier, plus it has shown the most activity."

"Are we flying?" Devon asked.

"Not quite. You will need to travel through a portal."

Vampie groaned. "Back to the cramped doghouse?"

"No, that was a small portal that leads to Osidian and back. There are stronger portals that allow travel around the world."

"How many are there?" Lobo asked.

"I know of about thirty large portals on Earth, including one in San Francisco. There are also hundreds of smaller ones. One of the large portals is only a few yards away from where we're standing."

"There's a portal here?"

"Yes. It's the reason I built my base and training center at this location."

Cornelius led them further down the corridor and through a metallic door. An Olympic sized swimming pool filled the room. The back wall and part of the roof were made of colored glass and mirrors.

Cornelius stopped at the edge of the water.

"Where is it?" Devon asked.

"In the center of the pool."

Lobo's face turned white. "I can't swim."

"No need. You only need to fall to the bottom, right at the center, and you'll travel through the portal," Cornelius explained.

Lobo's voice trembled. "But I still have to swim down there."

"I suppose you do, Jeremiah."

Devon sighed. She lifted Lobo by his shirt and belt and started swinging him.

"Devon, don't. Please!"

Devon threw Lobo in and he landed dead center. His arms and legs thrashed as he sank straight down. He yelled, but he was a moment too late as water flowed into his lungs.

"Please let this be quick," he thought to himself.

Lobo closed his eyes and stopped struggling long enough to realize he had just exhaled. His mouth and insides were full of water, but he was able to breathe. He heard a splash as Vampie and Devon followed him in. Lobo floated down and saw a small drain at the bottom of the pool. A light glowed near the drain, then turned into a bright circle that expanded as Lobo passed through it.

CHAPTER ELEVEN: BAY WATCH

The trio reappeared in a dark room.

Lobo was gasping. "Why did you push me?" he asked Devon, although he could only see the faint glow of her eyes.

"You're alive, aren't you?"

"I could have drowned."

"I knew it was breathing water. It's common in Osidian and most of the celestial worlds."

"She's correct, Lobo," Vampie said. "If you know what to look for, they're obvious. There are small, dark blue specks in the water that carry pockets of air. They provide enough oxygen to breathe and remain fully submerged and dry almost instantly once you're out of the water."

Lobo calmed down as he realized that he wasn't dripping wet and they were sitting in the dark. "Where are we? I can't see anything."

"Hold on," Devon said as she felt around. "We're in a thin enclosure." Her hand glowed and something clicked. A second later they were shot out into the daylight, landing on the ground.

Lobo looked up from the direction they came from. "There's nothing there but a brick wall."

"Clever," Devon said. "The portal's encased in that wall to disguise it. I felt something sticking out. It must have been a release latch."

"How are we going to get back in?" Lobo asked.

"Let's worry about that when we have to," Devon said.

Vampie was rubbing his rear. "They could have put a pillow or something for the landing."

"Have you all arrived safely?" Lobo and Vampie winced as their ears were filled with the loud crackling sound of Cornelius's voice. Devon looked unnerved.

Lobo poked his ear. "These communicators are really loud."

They heard a high-pitched whine and then nothing.

"That should be better."

"Yes, much," Lobo replied. "So this is San Francisco?"

"You're actually in an alley in Chinatown."

Vampie scratched his nose. "China? I thought San Francisco was in the United States. I need new Earth geography books."

"The books are fine, Vampire. Chinatown is in San Francisco. It's an area of the city where many people of Chinese descent live. You need to get from Chinatown to a building near the Fisherman's Wharf. The best way is to go by streetcar since it travels around the entire area."

"Oh, no," Vampie said as he realized they were out in the open and he hadn't transformed. He mumbled his magic words and was a Chihuahua again, wearing a thin sweater that held his belongings in Baron's collapsing kit.

"Do I have to change my hair again?" Devon asked.

"That's fine, just as long as your angelic features aren't visible," Cornelius answered.

Devon let her wings shrink until only a small bulge showed underneath her clothes. "What is a streetcar, anyway?"

"They are box shaped cars that are part of an electric transportation system," Cornelius explained. "They travel on rails and have stops throughout the city. They've been around for over a hundred years and are a major tourist attraction."

"Thanks for the lesson," Devon said. "How do we get there?"

"You need to head east and find a streetcar stop. Jeremiah, check your survival kit for a pair of sunglasses."

Lobo pulled his kit out of his pocket. It expanded and he reached in. "It's empty."

"You need to tell it what you're looking for," Devon reminded him.

Lobo raised the bag to his lips and whispered, "Sunglasses."

He reached in again and felt something in his hands. He pulled out a small piece of plastic that looked like a single lens. He pulled the lens apart and it opened up into full-size glasses. He put them on.

The right lens formed into a computer-like readout, showing Lobo an electronic map of their location. "Whoa."

"Follow the markings on the map," Cornelius instructed. "It will guide you to the streetcar and your destination. Just remember that you're supposed to be normal kids hanging out with your ugly, hairless dog."

Vampie growled.

Lobo led them out of the alley and they passed several shops and restaurants. They moved through the crowds without being noticed. Vampie stayed by Devon's side most of the time but stopped occasionally to look through gift shop windows and stare at the items out on the sidewalks. Within twenty minutes, they were out of Chinatown and approaching a streetcar stop.

Only one other person was standing at the stop. The three of them had never seen a live streetcar before and were staring at the car heading their way.

"So primitive," Devon said. "How does it work?"

"The wires above give the streetcars the energy to move," Baron broke in over their communicators. "The cars have long metal conductors that pull in the electricity and then use that power to move along the rails."

"Do we take this car?" Lobo asked.

"There should be a map somewhere that tells you which cars go to the Fisherman's Wharf," Cornelius said.

Lobo checked and found a map in the plastic casing around the bench stop. "We need to take the one marked 'F-Market and Wharves.'"

The approaching streetcar looked like a mini-bus. The banner over the front window was marked "M".

"Not this one," Lobo said.

A few passengers exited and the man that was waiting with them got on. Another streetcar followed a few minutes later.

"This is it."

This car was larger with yellow trim. They boarded, but the driver stopped Lobo as he tried to pass and pointed at a price list. "You need to pay first. That price is for each of you for a one-way trip. You'll have to hold on to the dog."

Lobo reached into his bag. "Money," he whispered. Several bills appeared and he handed over the cash.

They weaved through the city, passing glass buildings and hotels as they rolled up and down the hills of San Francisco, stopping every few minutes to pick up and drop off passengers. Lobo had traveled around the country with his parents, but he was a toddler and didn't remember much more than riding in the car. The city sights were as fascinating to him as they were to Devon and Vampie.

As they neared the water of San Francisco Bay, the buildings disappeared. They saw ships and passed a dock filled with boats. The streetcar stopped again.

Lobo walked up to the driver. His sunglasses map showed their destination was nearby. "Is this the main stop for the Fisherman's Wharf?"

The driver pointed over his head to a streetcar map. "There are a couple of more stops for the wharf, but this one is right in the middle of everything."

"Go ahead and get off here," Cornelius instructed over the communicators.

Lobo motioned to Devon and they jumped off the streetcar.

They crossed the street to a line of shops and buildings nearest the water.

"You are less than a mile from your target, Jeremiah," Cornelius said. "Before you proceed, go into the first gift shop you can find."

Lobo walked a few yards before finding a big gift shop with clothes and caps in the window. A small sign on the door read "NO PETS ALLOWED."

"Stay with Vampie, Devon. I won't be long."

Lobo entered the shop and checked out a wall of magnets. "Cornelius, what do I buy?"

"Anything that will help make you look like regular tourists."

Lobo looked over the baseball caps. He liked to feel his hair blowing in the wind and didn't wear caps often. Kyle was the cap wearer. Lobo figured he would be able to give it to him when he got back to the Academy. He found an adjustable grey cap with "San Francisco" written on the front and grabbed it. Next to the caps were mini baseballs and footballs and assorted toys. Lobo grabbed a Frisbee for Vampie.

He looked for a cap for Devon, but it didn't seem like her style. He looked through the store but couldn't settle on anything. He walked to the checkout where there were glass cases forming a rectangle. A pair of earrings stood out. They held small, oval shaped crystals that reminded him of Osidian. He asked the clerk to see a pair. Each crystal had an "SF" etched in them.

"I'll take these," Lobo said as he reached into his bag for money.

Lobo put on his cap, walked out of the store and found Devon and Vampie staring in the same direction.

"What?" Lobo asked.

"That bridge over the water. It's so grand," Devon said.

Lobo looked up and saw the Golden Gate Bridge. He had only seen it in pictures, but they didn't compare to seeing the real thing.

"There's no time for sightseeing. Time to move," Cornelius barked over the communicators.

The three of them snapped back.

"Keep going in the same direction and try to look normal."

"Here, before I forget," Lobo said as he handed Devon the earrings.

She looked them over. "Nice choice."

Lobo looked at her ears. "Your ears aren't pierced. I'm sorry, I didn't even think about it."

"You're an Earth boy," Devon said. "Of course you didn't think about it. Don't worry. I can fix that."

Devon looked at the people walking by, but no one paid them any notice. She lifted an earring to her lobe and a small hole burned open just enough for her to push it in.

She repeated the process for the other ear and then shook her head, letting the dangling earrings bounce around.

"Well?" she asked.

"Looks good," Lobo replied. Vampie yelped an approval.

They continued down the Wharf and passed one of the boat docks.

"You're close," Cornelius said. Lobo saw that they were almost on top of the blip on the sunglasses map. "There should be a two-story building in front of you."

Lobo raised his palm and, tapped it twice and aimed the camera forward.

"That yellow one?" he asked.

"Yes. Find a way over there, but make it look natural. Remember what you learned in the stealth simulator."

"This is for you, Vampie," Lobo said as he pulled out the Frisbee. He threw it hard and it flew in the direction of the building.

Vampie watched it fly.

"You're supposed to chase it," Lobo explained.

Vampie's head snapped and he ran after the toy. He tried to grab it with his paws.

Lobo shook his head. He took off his cap and bit into it, holding it up with his teeth so Vampie could see. The Chihuahua barked and then picked the Frisbee up with his teeth and ran back to his companions.

"That's it," Lobo said. "Now, go long."

Lobo threw the Frisbee behind the building. It landed near some doors facing the water and Vampie dashed to retrieve it with Lobo and Devon running after him. No one was outside, but they noticed security cameras over each door.

They reached Vampie and got a better look at the door directly in front of them. The camera was still and pointed at the door to view anyone going in or out. Vampie trotted closer to the door, but not close enough for the camera to see. Devon and Lobo followed. Devon casually lifted her hand and aimed at the camera, but Lobo tapped her shoulder. "No magic, remember? Now that we're this close, they may be able to detect it."

Devon stretched her fingers and then moved her hand to play with one of her new earrings, just in case someone was watching.

Lobo took the Frisbee from Vampie's mouth and tossed it. "Go get it, boy."

The Frisbee hit the camera and shifted it upwards. Lobo ran up to the door and tried the knob.

"We're at the door, Cornelius," Lobo whispered. "It's locked."

"Baron should have supplied you with a lock pick."

"But won't they be able to detect the magic?" Lobo asked.

"Good thinking, but it's not magic, Jeremiah. It's Baron's science and engineering."

Lobo took out his pouch. "Lockpick."

He pulled out a thin metal cylinder that was about as long as his index finger.

"Hold it up to the lock," Cornelius instructed.

Devon picked up Vampie and stroked his head, much to Vampie's discomfort. She stood in front of Lobo and used Vampie to block the view of anyone that might walk by.

Lobo bent down and pointed one end of the pick to the lock. The end of the cylinder clicked open and a bunch of thin threads emerged, extending into the lock's crevices. The threads felt around the lock's grooves and then stiffened. He felt the pick's weight increase as the threads twisted, unlocking the door. No alarms went off.

The three entered the building. They looked in each of the eight rooms but didn't find anyone or anything of interest.

"It doesn't look like there's anything here," Lobo said.

"My sensor's show you're in the right place," Cornelius said. "Unless it's a decoy. Check your glasses."

Lobo checked the computer readout and they were standing in the main blip. "It looks like we're in the right spot."

There was a loud crash. Lobo turned and saw Vampie crawling out of a trash can he had knocked over. As Lobo looked to the ground, the blip brightened.

"Hold on," Lobo said. He looked to each side of the room and then to the ceiling before taking a slow look down.

"Cornelius, the glasses get brighter when I look at the floor."

"Interesting. I'm checking with Baron."

They heard beeps and mumbled conversation over the communicators.

"It looks like you're in the proper location," Cornelius explained. "You just might be too high."

"Too high?"

"We never thought to check for depth. We just looked at the signals. However, it seems that your target is underground. Wait a few seconds. Baron's going to send an update to your glasses."

Devon pulled out her own glasses to see what was happening.

"Okay, Lobo. Check now."

The computer blip Lobo had been following changed from a flat block into a three-dimensional circle over a bigger block. The blip was now underneath them.

"The signal's about two hundred feet below you, but I

don't see a way down from your location. Baron's checking our master system."

They waited a few more seconds.

"Baron's found an entrance, but it's under water."

"I told you I can't swim," Lobo said.

"You probably won't have to. Most creatures from the demon realms don't do well in water, either. It sizzles their scales until they fall off."

"Demon sunburn?" Lobo asked.

"Only it burns enough to reach their bones. There's a tunnel of some kind that leads into the area. It runs several miles into the Bay and we've seen only one land entrance."

Lobo and Devon saw the long tube in their glasses. Devon moved toward the window and looked out.

"It's that small island," she said, pointing.

"Alcatraz Island," Cornelius said. "You need to get to Alcatraz."

"Alcatraz?" Devon asked.

"It used to be a prison," Lobo answered. "But they closed it down a long time ago after a famous escape and because it was too expensive to keep open. I remember watching a movie about it and thinking I could escape from the Academy. Problem was, I didn't have anywhere to go."

"It's a tourist attraction now," Cornelius said. "However, unlike the streetcars, they do not allow pets unless it's for medical reasons. Cherub, if you are able, the Scribe may serve you better as a bird. Magic should be safe considering your target is below ground."

"I can come close," Devon said. "He has to be similar in size and shape. He'd be a rather large bird."

"Get it as close as you can. He needs to be able to fly or swim to the island. There are tour boats that can take you there. You are close to the pier where they depart, so you'll need to get tickets before the next one leaves. I'll have Baron update your maps."

Lobo checked his map as the new destination was added.

"Vampie, can you turn into any kind of bird?"

"I don't think I can form feathers," the vampire answered. "Devon, see what you can do."

Devon waved her hands and the Chihuahua sprouted featherless wings. His body thinned out some and his paws became claws. His ears shrunk to almost nothing, but otherwise, his face was unchanged.

"I can't get any feathers, either," Devon said. "The texture is too different from his normal body. The beak's not working, either."

"How about a bat?" Lobo asked. "I mean, he is a vampire."

Vampie gasped. "That is an insane Earth myth. Vampires do not turn into smelly, disgusting bats. I could be a fish instead."

"You might also get eaten before you make it to the island," Lobo said.

Vampie gave a firm nod. "A bat it is. I hope no one in my family ever hears of this. Please don't make me smelly."

Devon waved again and Vampie turned into a decent looking bat, but he was about the size of a cat. "Now try flying."

Vampie fluttered up and fell straight back on his head. He tried again but knocked over a lamp and shattered it. He tried a few more times until he was able to stay airborne.

"Better," Devon said. "Just fly along the boat and land on it if you feel like you're going to fall or if your wings get tired."

The three set off to the dock for the Alcatraz tours. Vampie flew nearby, running into a few signs and building rooftops along the way. People pointed at the unusual bat flying around during the daytime but left it alone.

Lobo bought two tickets and he and Devon boarded the ferry. The boat took a long route to Alcatraz. The tourists got a better view of the Golden Gate Bridge and the different parts of the island. The ferry docked and the pair walked into the main gate where they were greeted by a tour guide dressed in a park ranger uniform. The guide led them toward the main prison, stopping every few minutes to discuss its history.

Devon and Lobo stayed behind the group as Vampie flew above them.

"The entrance is in the prison," Cornelius said.

Vampie flew down to Devon and Lobo. "What do I do?"

Lobo pointed up. "Just stay high and out of sight."

The group entered the prison where most of the visitors decided to sign up for headsets and take an audio tour. Only a few people were without headphones, including Lobo and Devon.

"The ferry will leave right at six," the tour guide said. "Please be at the main entrance fifteen minutes beforehand."

The group dispersed. As most of the guests followed each other on the audio tour, Lobo and Devon broke free, following the blip on their map. Along the way, they blended with the tourists when they had to and learned of some of Alcatraz's most famous prisoners, such as the notorious gangster Al Capone and the Birdman of Alcatraz.

They also saw a cell with a fake dummy head that depicted how three prisoners made their famous escape. Their bodies were never found, so police were unable to prove whether they actually succeeded or if they just became shark bait. Lobo had to pull a captivated Devon away from the display.

The blip grew stronger as they reached the part of the prison called "The Hole." These were a set of cells where prisoners were sent to spend time alone in complete darkness as punishment.

"The entrance is here," Lobo whispered as he motioned for Vampie to fly down and join them.

Lobo moved to each cell. The blip got brighter on the third one.

"Here," he said just as a few tourists walked in and Vampie ducked into one of the cells. They were taking the audio tour and paid no mind to the young boy and wannabe guardian angel searching for an entrance. They walked away after a few minutes.

"Hurry," Devon said.

They entered the cell. Lobo and Devon used their hands to feel along the walls and floor. "There's something on the ceiling," Vampie said. "My bat sonar is picking up something."

Lobo felt around. "There's a tiny hole here. I can't press it or anything."

Devon felt it and started to wave her fingers.

"No more magic. We're too close," Lobo warned.

Devon pulled back. She grabbed Vampie by the legs and held one of his claws like a pen. She rubbed his claw along the indentation. Vampie screeched as his head dangled.

Something snapped and a small hatch opened below them, revealing a ladder.

"Let's go before someone comes in," Lobo said.

They rushed down and Devon closed the hatch behind her.

Fifty feet later, they hit ground. Vampie flew beside

them. The damp ground moved downwards at a slight angle. It was dark at first, but lights appeared every few hundred feet that were bright enough for them to see ahead.

"Cornelius, we're moving down the tunnel, but haven't seen anything yet," Lobo said.

Static filled their ears.

"Cornelius, are you there?"

More static.

Vampie flew between his companions. "We're probably too far below ground to get a signal."

"Or something's blocking the signal," Devon said.

Lobo raised his palms forward and flexed his fingers. "I have the camera inside my hand. I'll record what I can. We need to try and leave some of the remote cameras if we get the chance."

"There's something ahead," Devon said.

Lobo squinted. "I don't see anything."

"I can see a lot further than humans and vampires. It's a Cherub thing."

As they moved closer, they saw several shipping crates. They ran into more than ten small tractor-like vehicles. The light at the end of the tunnel started to grow brighter when they heard something moving. They jumped behind the nearest crates.

Devon stuck her head out. "They're Korindian guards."

They stealthed from crate to crate until they had a clear view of the guards. Two were standing at attention while one walked back and forth. The tunnel opened into another section behind the guards.

"Now what?" Devon said.

Lobo stood up and threw his cap down. "I'll take care of them."

"This is just supposed to be recon," Devon said. "We

don't have any weapons. Vampie can fly past them and leave the tracking devices."

"I have my staff," Lobo replied. "They're just slow Korindians. I can take them out before anyone knows what's happened. We can get further inside."

"Then you'll do it alone," Devon huffed. "It's an unnecessary risk."

"I don't need your help. You saw how I handled them during training. I'll be back in less than two minutes."

CHAPTER TWELVE:
A RUDE AWAKENING

Lobo stepped out from behind the crates and walked toward the guards.

"Aren't you going after him?" Vampie asked.

"No, he doesn't need our help, remember?"

As Lobo approached, the Korindian who had been walking his beat noticed the intruder and headed straight to him.

"Are you lost, boy?" the Korindian asked.

"I found this weird door in Alcatraz and wanted to see where it went. Cool costume. Is this part of the tour?"

"You need to leave now. This area is private."

Lobo moved closer. The Korindian's chest groaned with every breath as mucus dripped down its fat nostrils. It was bigger than the one in the training room and smelled like a rotting fish.

The other two guards moved behind the one speaking with Lobo and held their weapons in a ready position.

"We are not wearing costumes. Your worst nightmares can't compare to what we really are. Just leave now before we make you go."

Sweat started pouring down Lobo's forehead. In the training room, he wasn't worried about getting hurt when the worst that could happen was getting a slight shock.

Lobo's lips were trembling. "I-I'm not afraid of you."

The Korindian raised his spear, then threw it aside. "No need for weapons. You will learn what fear is."

The guard lunged. Lobo's instincts kicked in and he sidestepped, but his stomach was still full of razor-winged butterflies and he wanted to throw up. He felt movement behind him and ducked as the guard swung. Lobo lifted his hands to strike, but couldn't feel his fingers. The guard clocked him on top of his head and pushed him hard. Lobo flew back and slid near the crates where Devon and Vampie were hiding.

"Stop while you still have life," the guard warned.

The other two guards moved forward.

"No," the guard yelled. "I will teach him the respect he lacks."

Vampie clawed at Devon's shoulder. "He's going to get killed. We have to help him."

Devon cracked her knuckles. "I guess it would look bad if my first charge didn't make it through his inaugural mission." She stared at Lobo. "Reckless boy. You're lucky I'm up for a fight."

She stepped out in the open just as Vampie took flight and knocked over a crate, hitting the Cherub on the head. She was dazed and fell down as Vampie flew off, unaware of what he had done.

"What was that noise?" one of the guards asked.

They saw Vampie fly by.

"Just a bat," the head guard replied.

Lobo got up and stepped forward. The guard rushed him, but he dashed out of the way. The guard tripped over

Lobo's foot and fell face down.

"Not bad for a child, am I?" Lobo crowed, just a moment before a second guard hit him from behind. The head guard got up and kicked Lobo in the stomach. The other two guards joined in, punching and kicking the boy.

The lead guard raised his head. "Enough. If we kill him, we might draw more unwelcome visitors."

The guard knelt down and stuck his wet snout against Lobo's nose.

"You got in a fight with other boys, do you understand? If you tell anyone about this, we'll come after you and your family. I'm sure you're all quite tasty."

Lobo could barely see through his swollen eyes but managed to nod.

"Go back the way you came. I'll give you ten minutes before we sweep back and seal that entrance."

Lobo lifted himself up and limped away. He saw Devon rubbing her head. Once the guards returned to their posts, she emerged with her arms crossed. "You really ripped them apart."

Lobo's head dropped. "I'm sorry, Devon. I made a big mistake."

Devon reached for his forehead. "Let me heal. . ."

"No. No magic still. Right now they think I was just some idiot kid that got lost."

"They got the idiot part right."

"I deserve this pain. It'll remind me not to do anything that stupid again. Can I lean on you?"

Devon wrapped Lobo's arm around her and helped him along.

"Where's Vampie?" he asked.

Devon turned back. "I'm not sure. He flew away just when I was going to get into some real action."

Almost on cue, they heard fluttering. Vampie landed on

Devon's shoulder.

"Did you lose a quill?" Devon asked. "First, you knocked me on the head with a crate and then you missed Lobo's impression of a punching bag. This mission was a complete waste."

"I wouldn't say complete," Vampie said. "While Lobo was in battle, I made it past everyone and planted Baron's cameras. My apologies about the crate, Devon."

"What was back there?" Devon asked.

"More crates and tunnels. Some led to another underground area," Vampie answered. "There were more Korindians digging with shovels and riding those tractors."

"At least this wasn't a total loss," Lobo said.

The three made their way back to the Alcatraz ferry. Lobo left his sunglasses on and kept his head down to avoid any attention.

The communicators still didn't work, so they returned to the Chinatown alley still unsure of how to get through the brick wall. Devon and Vampie the Chihuahua discussed it as Lobo sat on the ground.

"Maybe we need to blow it up," Vampie suggested.

"What would be the point of hiding it then?"

"I'm sure Cornelius knows."

"We can't speak to him, though, can we, vampire dog?"

Devon threw rocks against the wall, but nothing happened. "Forget this. I can get us out of here."

The vampire was curious. "How? Do you know of another portal?"

"No. I need a sleeping child. A baby, if possible. It just needs to be in a place where we won't be seen."

Her answer shocked Lobo. "Are you planning on kidnapping a baby?"

"Of course not. Just help me find one."

They left the alley and searched down the street. They

saw several children sleeping in strollers, but there were too many people out in the open.

After a few more minutes, Lobo stopped and pointed. "Does that say 'Child Care' or 'Underwear'? I still can't see that well."

Devon looked up. "It's 'Child Care.' Let's go." She led them through a side entrance. "More stealth," she said.

She checked the door, but it was locked. She waved her hand, the lock snapped open and she turned the handle.

The trio walked in and heard children laughing and playing as they moved through a short hall. The windows had crayon drawings and nursery rhyme characters covering most of them. Devon was able to look into the cracks between the pictures, but all of the rooms were filled with kids that were wide awake. A door closed behind them.

They ducked behind a wall as footsteps came closer.

"Are they all asleep?" a woman's voice asked.

"Looks like it. I love naptime," another woman answered.

The steps came closer. Devon held her arm out and shut her eyes. A dark glow surrounded the three. The women walked by and one turned toward them, then went right back to her conversation.

Lobo was stunned.

"I made a protection bubble around us and we blended into the shadows," Devon said.

They moved toward the room where the kids were napping. A sign on the door read "Nursery." Devon turned the knob and peeked inside. An older lady sat at a desk and was reading a book. Sleeping children filled several cribs and small beds.

Devon raised her hand. "Stay close." A dark bubble surrounded them again.

The lady at the desk got up to check the open door. As she looked down the hall, the three entered and moved to the back of the room. The woman walked in and returned to her desk.

Devon moved toward one of the beds where a small boy was sleeping. "Okay, you ready?" she said in her normal tone.

Lobo and Vampie jumped.

"It's okay," Devon said. "The bubble's soundproof. We can scream if we want to, but we don't want to wake the child."

Lobo was still confused. "What are we doing here, Devon?"

"We're going back to see Cornelius. As close as we can get, at least."

Vampie pointed to the baby. "The child's a portal?"

"No. Another advantage to being part angel is that we can travel through dreams."

"Then why didn't we just use that homeless man in the alley?" Lobo asked.

"It doesn't work that way. Whenever small children dream, they can speak to angels. The children are still uncorrupted by the world, so they get a direct line to the heavens. When you see a child laughing or yawning as they sleep, the angels are probably with them."

"I always thought that just meant they had gas," Lobo said. "How do we get in their dreams?"

"We're not actually going into their dreams. We're just piggy-backing on the connection. We'll start with this boy and hopefully end with another dreaming child that's located near the training facility. We might see parts of the dreams as we go, so don't freak. Keep a hand on me."

Lobo grabbed her arm and Vampie put a paw on her foot. Devon placed the fingers of one hand over the other and set her palms on the child's head. Her hair flowed as a soft wind blew and the three of them shot up as if being sucked into the sky.

Lobo couldn't see anything for a few moments but felt as if he was floating and a silent fan was blowing him forward. He felt at peace as he breathed in a sweet smelling aroma. He noticed Devon and Vampie next to him as soft clouds surrounded them and formed images. One cloud was an angel holding a baby and kissing him on the forehead. Large milk bottles danced above them. A woman, the baby's mother, Lobo guessed, snuggled him against her shoulder. A bright flash of light surrounded them. Their white surroundings changed into bright neon colors. A different child dressed in pink was rising and falling as a Cherub, whose skin and clothes were all bright blue, tossed her into the air. The baby laughed and spit up in the angel's face, causing her to laugh even harder. Three other angels floated above the laughing child. The baby turned to them and babbled in their direction. The angels laughed and babbled right back.

Lobo's body twitched as bright colors popped like balloons. The three were standing by a baby girl asleep in a crib. She was still babbling.

"That was incredible," Lobo said. "Where are we?"

"We're in a neighborhood near the training facility," Devon answered. "It was the closest I could get."

They moved within the bubble to the next room and saw the child's mother folding clothes. They turned and left through a back door in the kitchen.

The bubble faded as they walked into the daylight.

"Why don't you keep us covered?" Lobo asked.

"It only works in low light."

Lobo wanted to ask more but was interrupted by the blip in his glasses. "We're still more than five miles from the training center."

Devon shrugged. "I guess we'll just have to walk."

After only a short stroll, a black limousine screeched toward them. The stocky driver got out of the car and held the door open.

"Cornelius knows we're back," Devon said.

They were in the training room within minutes.

"I take it the communicators stopped working," Cornelius said as they entered the room.

Devon and Vampie nodded.

Lobo felt his wounds throbbing. His face grew hotter the longer he looked at his grandfather and he could only think of the beating he had just endured.

"Fortunately, we were able to track your signals," Cornelius continued. "We also saw that you were able to plant tracking cameras at the site."

"Yes," Lobo said, gritting his teeth. "We're done. I want to go home now."

Cornelius moved closer. "It appears you took on an enemy. It didn't go well, I take it?"

Lobo exploded. "No, it didn't go well! I was almost killed because your lousy Gornda didn't even come close to what the Korindians were really like!"

"Angel, can you not heal him?" Cornelius asked.

"He wouldn't let me."

"Jeremiah, let her help you."

Lobo looked away and didn't answer. Devon walked up to him and cradled his face with her hands. The swelling shrunk and the throbbing pain in his side disappeared.

"I still need you," Cornelius said.

"You said we just had to do recon. You have the cameras. I quit." Lobo stormed off and headed back to the exit.

Cornelius hovered to the door and cut his grandson off.

"Jeremiah, I need to tell you something important. If you still want to leave afterward, I'll respect that. I need you, but will not force you to stay. I know you must have been frightened, but you weren't ready to fight. You were just supposed to gather information. Please, I must speak with you privately."

Lobo stared at the ground and breathed through his teeth as he followed Cornelius to a room near Baron's workshop.

"Nothing you say is going to matter," Lobo said. "I want to know more about my parents, but I'm not going to die for that."

"Does the name Micah Dukane mean anything to you?"

Lobo shook his head.

"We have heard his name mentioned several times since the cameras came online. Dukane is a powerful businessman with big ties to the Earth underground. He also has knowledge of the celestial and demon realms. We suspect he is the person responsible for the fire that killed your mother and father."

Lobo looked up and didn't say anything for a long time. Finally, he let out a deep breath and looked back at the ground. "What does it matter? Even if we catch him, my parents are still dead."

Cornelius paused. "It's true your mother was killed in the fire. However, there is something you don't know, Jeremiah Coronado. Your father, The Grey Wolf, is still very much alive."

CHAPTER THIRTEEN: FAMILY CONNECTIONS

Lobo stared at his grandfather. "That's not true."

"It is, Jeremiah. Sebastian survived the fire. I pulled him out of the burning building myself. It took more than a year for me to recover and the only way I was able to get around was due to Baron's genius in designing this chair. Your father's injuries were much worse. His mind suffered more damage than his body ever did and he's still healing."

"Why didn't you tell me this before?"

"To protect you and your father. He isn't in a position to protect himself and if his enemies found out that either of you were alive, they would probably hunt you both down."

"Then why tell me now?"

"Because the Zaan could mean the destruction of life as we know it on Earth. It is too important and I truly believe we need you. Telling you this is putting you in danger, but you're not leaving me much of a choice."

"What's wrong with my father's mind?"

"He's not completely aware of who he is. He's in a

different reality."

"Does he remember me?"

"I'm not sure."

"What about this Dukane? Why do you think he tried to kill my family?"

"We found a card with the Dukane company logo in the ashes. Although no one was able to prove it, this was Dukane's calling card – something he would leave behind. Your father was investigating him and had found something big. He called me to discuss it, but the fire was burning strong by the time I arrived."

"Are you sure it was him?"

"I would bet my fortune on it," Cornelius said. "If he was the one who set the fire, he didn't care that you and your mother were inside. Now, I'm giving you a chance to help stop the man who destroyed your family."

Lobo thought for a long moment, trying to register everything.

"I want to see my father."

"Absolutely not. You'd increase the chance that he'd be discovered."

"I don't care. You might be my grandfather, but I just met you. How do I know you're not just telling me this to get me to stay?"

"You have no way of knowing for sure. You'll just have to trust me. When this is over, you can see him as often as you'd like."

"No. I see him now or I go back to the Academy. The only person I really trust is there."

Cornelius's face turned red and his nostrils flared.

"You are as stubborn as your father. I'll take you, but there is one condition. You cannot tell Devon or the vampire."

"Why?" Lobo asked.

"You have only known them a few hours less than you have known me. How can you trust them? The more beings that have this information, the greater the chance an enemy will find out."

"Okay, I won't tell them. Can we go now?"

They returned to the training room where Devon and Vampie were still waiting.

"What happened?" Devon asked. "Are we going back to Mr. Kindly's house?"

"No," Lobo replied. "I have to go somewhere with Cornelius. Alone."

Devon's forehead wrinkled. "And what are we supposed to do?"

"You have the Gornda and the training room all to yourself," Cornelius said. "We won't be long."

"How am I supposed to chronicle what's happened?" Vampie asked.

Devon shook her head slowly as she stared Lobo down. "You'll have to hope Mr. Secret fills you in later. So much for being a team."

She turned on her heels and headed for the weapons. "I need to hit something."

Lobo and Cornelius left the building. Vampie stood silently as they left.

Cornelius and Lobo met the waiting car. As the driver held the door open, Lobo noticed Cornelius's chair was too wide to fit in the door.

"How are you going to get in?"

Cornelius didn't answer. The driver raised his hand to stop Lobo from entering the vehicle. Cornelius's chair hovered close to the door, then four mechanical arms rose from it and pulled his body out of the machine. The old man had metallic stumps where his legs should be that looked like pipes with rounded ends. The arms then lifted his body into the car. Part of the backseat flipped and whirred, revealing a seat with holes in it. Cornelius's body eased into the seat until his leg stumps and torso snapped into place. The driver then opened the trunk and stored the chair inside.

Lobo joined his grandfather in the car. "Does it hurt?" he asked.

"Not as much as it used to," Cornelius said. "I've learned to function with the pain. Most of my nerve endings in my legs and lower body were burned, but there are still enough left to remind me of the fire. Baron's creations have helped keep me useful."

"What about my father? Is he in a mechanical chair, too?"

"No, I pulled you and your father out with enough time. He only suffered minor burns, but he was severely beaten before the house was torched. I was going back in for your mother, but the roof fell on me. I suspect she was killed before the fire got to her, but we'll never know."

Lobo lowered his head. "There wasn't enough left of her, was there?"

Cornelius didn't reply, but Lobo knew he was right.

The youngest Coronado stared out the window and thought of his parents and how horribly they suffered. He wondered why he wasn't more excited that he was about to meet his father, but he knew the answer. Fear consumed him. He was afraid that Cornelius was lying and he was headed for one of the most disappointing moments in his life. Hardly a day went by that he hadn't wished he could see his mother and father again. That wish was granted only a few days before in Osidian through the eyes of Thornos, but this was different.

They traveled for almost thirty minutes, but it seemed like hours to Lobo. His body was sweating as he thought of what he might say to his father.

"We're here," Cornelius said.

They pulled up to a hospital. Cornelius picked up a phone and dialed a number.

"It's me. I need to see him."

The car maneuvered toward the back of the hospital. They passed the emergency room exit and then approached a long ramp that sloped downwards. As the car neared, a garage door opened.

"This is where they receive their shipments," Cornelius explained. "I have to come in a back way. I tend to draw attention with my chair."

The car entered the door and rode down to an empty shipping area. The driver retrieved the hover chair and Cornelius was lifted out of the car and back into his craft.

"Come with me, Jeremiah."

Lobo followed Cornelius up a few staircases and through several doors. They walked down a long hallway and made a few turns. Cornelius stopped in front of a set of double doors. The sign read "Morgue."

Lobo's heart fell into his stomach. "So, he is dead."

"If you were searching for someone, would this be one of the first places you'd look?"

Cornelius entered the doors and Lobo followed.

There were several covered bodies on slabs. One body was under lamps and exposed as if the coroner walked out in the middle of inspecting it. Cornelius moved toward the back of the room to a single door. It had a small keypad in front of it. Cornelius entered some numbers and the door unlocked. This led to a smaller ramp and a long hallway. They faced three doors, and Cornelius opened the middle one. The room was a storage closet filled with brooms, cleaning supplies and assorted containers. Cornelius squeezed his chair through.

"Close the door behind you, Jeremiah."

Cornelius pulled out a small object that looked like a flashlight. He flipped it on and it emitted a green beam of light. He aimed it at the back of the cramped room where various tools hung. Lobo heard a snap and the tool rack split apart, revealing another opening. They entered into a larger area that held one last door. It was wide and contained a small, dark window with a metal slit underneath it. A man in a white coat was waiting.

"Dr. Jansen," Cornelius said. "This is Jeremiah Coronado. He's here to see his father."

The doctor froze for a moment, then shook Lobo's hand. "Hello, Jeremiah. I didn't realize you were alive. Your father has mentioned your name a few times, but he usually calls you Lobo."

"My father's mentioned me?"

"He speaks in bits and pieces. He may go months without saying a word, and then he'll talk nonstop for days."

"Can I see him?"

Dr. Jansen looked up at Cornelius. "Alone?"

"Is he restrained?" Cornelius asked.

"Not now. Give me a moment."

The doctor opened the door and entered. Lobo tried to peek in, but couldn't see anything.

"Why do they have to restrain him?" Lobo asked his grandfather.

"He might think he's in the middle of a fight and start to attack anyone near him, even his own son."

The doctor returned a few minutes later.

"He's ready for you," the doctor said. "Although he's tied down, you need to watch yourself. Don't get too close."

Lobo closed his eyes as he entered the room. He felt his

heart banging against his chest and every vein in his head pulsating.

A bed was on one side of the room. It didn't have any sheets and had one pillow without a case. The walls were cushioned, but otherwise bare. There were no windows, pictures, or electronic devices of any kind. Lobo's sneakers squeaked as he stopped cold. He was fixated on a man seated on a metal bench across the room, facing away from him. The man was still, but Lobo could hear him breathing. As Lobo got closer, he saw that the man's arms were bound with straps attached to each end of the bench.

Lobo walked around to face him and get a better look, but the man's hair was long and covered his features. He kept his distance as Dr. Jansen instructed, but fought the urge to reach over and lift the man's hair out of the way.

"Excuse me," Lobo said. "Are you Sebastian Coronado?"

The man didn't respond.

"Does the Grey Wolf mean anything to you?"

The man's head tilted and his hair split enough to reveal part of his face.

"Wolf," the man said. "Grey Wolf."

Lobo's insides tightened as he recognized the eyes. "Father?"

His hands were shaking as he did his best to keep from rushing and embracing him.

"Father," the man repeated. "My father is Cornelius."

"Yes, Cornelius is your father, but you are my father."

The man didn't react.

"I'm Jeremiah. Your son."

The man looked to each side of the room and ducked to check under the bed.

"The walls whisper," he said. "Demons are everywhere."

"They're not here, Father. It's just us."

"I kill demons."

"I know. Do you remember your wife, Kira?"

"I have to stop them," the man continued. "I have to stop him."

Lobo's head fell. "I want you to hear something before I go, even if you don't remember." His voice cracked. "Lobo Coronado, your son, loves you and misses you."

"Lobo?" the man said as his eyes watered. "Lobo. My son." Sebastian Coronado's eyes widened and locked on his face for a long moment.

"Yes," Lobo said with all doubts now erased. "I'm your son. I'm Lobo, Dad."

"My boy," Sebastian moved toward his son, but his restraints held him back. Lobo didn't hesitate. He wrapped his arms around his father and was overcome with cries of joy.

"I've missed you so much, Dad. I thought you were dead."

Sebastian's body stiffened and Lobo let go.

"My Lobo," he said through gritted teeth. "He killed my Lobo. Dukane made my family dead."

Sebastian screamed as if his heart was being ripped out. He jumped off the bench and it groaned as the restraints stretched. Sebastian started swinging his arms and although the bench was attached to the ground, one of the legs cracked and an arm restraint snapped free.

The doctor ran in. "Lobo, you need to leave now. Hurry."

Lobo couldn't move. The doctor grabbed him by the shirt and pulled him back. Sebastian clenched his fists and pulled himself up harder. The legs of the bench broke apart.

The doctor ran out of the room and slammed the door

shut behind him. A loud crash hit the door and the window shattered as the bench slammed into it.

"It's okay now, Lobo." The doctor was shaking.

"He recognized me, Doctor," Lobo said. "Only for a second, but he knew me."

"I think he did," the doctor said. "It's difficult for him to control himself. He can go months without expressing emotion and then one day break into an uncontrollable rage. It has been more than a year since that's happened. That could have been you thrown against that door instead of the bench."

"Why is he like this?" Lobo asked.

"The trauma from being beaten and burned damaged him," the doctor answered. "He lives in his memories and doesn't seem able to move on."

"Will he ever get better?"

A loud bang made them all jump. Sebastian started pounding against the door and more glass pieces shattered.

"Open this!" he yelled. "Have to go to Texas. Have to get to Dukane."

Dr. Jansen opened a keypad panel by the door and hit some buttons. Sebastian's pounding stopped and a blue mist seeped from the cracked window.

"Step away from the door," the doctor said. "I've released a tranquilizer gas that should calm him for a few hours. If any of us breathe it in, we'll be out for days."

Lobo moved back. "Will it hurt him?"

"No. I only use the gas in emergencies. The first time this happened, he continued pounding on the doors and padded walls until he broke every bone in his hands. After that, we added ten times the normal padding and secured his bench and bed several feet into the ground. It looks like we'll have to find something stronger."

"Do what you must," Cornelius said. "Jeremiah, it's

time to leave."

Cornelius took some time before asking Lobo about what had happened. They were halfway to the training compound before he spoke. "What's going through your mind?"

"He thought I was dead. You should have told him. You should have told me."

"I'm still not convinced I've done the right thing. What would happen if even one of your father's enemies knew he was in this state and his son was alive?"

"Do you think Dukane would come after him if he knew?"

"I don't know. He may not consider him a threat anymore. At least now we're sure it is Dukane."

"What do you mean?"

"He said Dukane killed his family. He's never said that before. I think seeing you spurred his memory and threw him into a rage."

"He's never mentioned Dukane before today?"

"Yes, but he talks about many enemies, and he usually just rambles into meaningless phrases. This time he was specific. He also mentioned Texas, which does contain one of the hotspots we've been monitoring. Now I'm even more convinced it was Dukane all along."

"What happens now?"

"That depends on your answer to the question I'm about to ask. Now you know that I told you the truth about your father being alive. Dukane appears to be behind the Zaan, but the Grey Wolf isn't around to stop him. What I need to know, Grandson, is what do you intend to do?"

Lobo stared out the window, took in a deep breath and then locked his eyes on his grandfather.

"Revenge. I want revenge."

"Very well, Jeremiah," Cornelius said. "Those are

dangerous words, but you have every right to speak them. Dukane also put me in this chair. We need to trust each other if we're going to succeed."

"Whatever it takes," Lobo said as he stuck his hand out.

Cornelius took his grandson's hand and shook it.

"Whatever it takes."

CHAPTER FOURTEEN: TEXAS TROUBLE

Lobo entered the training room and found Devon on top of Vampie, holding a dagger to his neck.

"You need to worry about the weapon," Devon instructed. "Get it out of my hands or move your head out of the way."

Vampie's long fingers swished and knocked the dagger from Devon's grip.

"Better," Devon said. "You would have only died eight times this round."

Cornelius followed and the sound of his chair caught the Cherub's attention.

Devon returned the dagger to the weapon rack. "How was the field trip?"

Lobo ignored her question. "We're going to Texas to look for a man named Micah Dukane."

"Why the change of heart?"

Lobo hesitated and looked at Cornelius.

Devon rolled her eyes. "Fine, keep it to yourself. We're ready to go whenever you are, Boss."

"Are we going through the pool again?" Vampie asked.

"Yes," Cornelius said. "You're going to end up in a small town in North Texas. I'll have air transportation waiting to take you to your final destination in Dallas."

Lobo glared at Devon. "There's another way."

Devon flashed her scraping teeth.

"What way?" Cornelius asked.

Lobo felt Devon's stare piercing through his head. "It's just that I've never flown before. I was hoping we could drive."

"That will take too long, Jeremiah."

"Never mind then."

Baron refilled their supply bags with rations and they were soon back at the pool. Lobo sat at the edge of the water and eased in. Although he knew he couldn't drown, he held his breath until he passed through the portal.

The trio appeared in darkness but could see small strands of light around them.

Devon started to move toward the light, but Lobo put his hand on her shoulder. "Communicators off."

Their ears popped as the connection was severed.

"Why didn't you tell Cornelius about the dream travel?"

Devon bit her lip as she spoke. "He must have said something for you not to trust us. If you don't have to tell us where you were and why you changed your mind, then I don't have to tell him anything."

"Devon, I'm sorry."

"Breath waste."

Lobo started to speak, but thought of his father and snapped his mouth shut. "Let's just go."

Vampie sniffed a few times. "What is that smell?"

"I wasn't going to say anything," Devon said. "I thought it was you."

"I'll have you know, Devon, that vampires are one of

the cleanest creatures in all of Osidian."

Lobo took in a few whiffs. "I know what that is."

Devon and Vampie waited, but Lobo didn't say anything right away.

"Well?" the Cherub asked.

"Horses. There's a festival parade every year that passes near the Academy. You never forget the smell of horse dung."

"Dung?" Vampie said. "You mean they leave their internal mess in the streets?"

Lobo nodded. "I don't think they make bathrooms their size."

"Ugh. I'm definitely cleaner than anything on this planet."

Devon felt around the front wall and found a handle. She opened the door in front of her, revealing a horse's backside.

"It looks like we're in a stable," Lobo said.

They walked by a brown horse. It was eating and paid them no attention.

Lobo ran his hand across the horse's neck. Devon started to touch it but hesitated.

"It's okay," Lobo assured her. "They're big but usually friendly. At least the horses in the parades were. There aren't any horses in Osidian?"

Devon reached out and stroked the horse. "No, we have creatures that are similar, but they have snouts and tusks and attack you if you get too close."

"You want to try, Vampie?" Lobo asked.

No answer.

Lobo and Devon looked back at the vampire Scribe. He was staring at the horse. His eyes were wide and bulging out of their sockets. A thick vein in his neck was throbbing.

"What's wrong?" Lobo asked.

"I hadn't even thought about it," Devon said. "Vampie, you haven't had any blood since we've been here, have you?"

Vampie shook his head but kept staring at the horse as saliva dripped from his fangs.

"Vampires need to feed once every few days, Lobo. If they wait too long, they can be overcome with thirst."

"Will he kill it?" Lobo asked.

"No, he shouldn't. Although vampires can feed on almost any blood creature, their meal of choice is the corna. The corna generate too much blood and without a vampire's help, they'd swell up until their insides exploded. The feedings keep them alive."

"The horse could get spooked and go wild."

"I'll be gentle," Vampie whispered. "I won't hurt this beautiful, delicious looking beast."

Devon pulled Lobo out of the way.

Vampie leapt onto the horse's back. The horse kept feeding as he eased up the long neck. Vampie looked at his companions and smiled as his two upper fangs extended from his mouth. The teeth were longer and thinner than Lobo had seen in scary movies. Vampie let his teeth puncture the horse's neck with a gentle pop. The horse grunted but continued eating.

A few minutes passed and Vampie raised his head and let out a satisfied moan. His white fangs were red and he slurped a last, thick drop of blood as his teeth shrunk to their normal size.

"That was soooo good," Vampie sighed. "Much spicier than cornas."

Lobo finally blinked. "Remind me never to make you mad."

"Don't worry, Lobo. If I had to choose between death and drinking human blood, I'd go to my grave without hesitation."

"We should let Cornelius know we're okay," Lobo said. "Communicator's on."

"What took so long?" Cornelius asked.

"We were just having a snack. We're in a horse stable. What now?"

"Start heading east. Your transportation should be there any minute."

They walked past the other three horses in the stable and out to an open area of grass. A herd of cows grazed nearby. A farmhouse stood about a mile away, but other than the animals, no one else was around.

"What is this place?" Vampie asked.

"Looks like a big ranch," Lobo answered. "On a lazy day."

"You're standing on one of the largest ranches in the state," Cornelius stated over the communicators. "It's almost a million acres large."

A faint whirring filled the quiet air.

"What is that?" Devon asked.

"Your ride should be visible at any moment," Cornelius said.

The noise grew louder.

Vampie pointed toward the clouds. "There's a big bird headed this way."

"That's not a bird. It's a helicopter," Lobo said.

"It's a flying machine?"

"Yes. You don't have them on Osidian?"

Vampie shook his head. "In all my jobs over the centuries I learned to drive almost every kind of vehicle on Osidian, but not one of them could fly. We have other methods of getting around."

"You'll be in Dallas in about half an hour this way," Cornelius cut in.

"We're going in that?" Devon asked.

"I've never been on one before," Lobo said. "This should be cool."

The cows looked up and the horses in the stable stirred as the chopper landed. The sound of the blades was deafening, causing Vampie to hold his hands over his ears. Lobo ran toward the helicopter as the pilot walked out to greet them.

"I'm Tim," he said. "I'll get you strapped in. You'll have to hold your dog."

Lobo turned and saw Vampie had transformed. He wondered if the pilot knew of otherworldly creatures, considering his grandfather had hired him.

"Come on, Vampie." The dog jumped into Lobo's arms.

Tim strapped them in and took off. Lobo's stomach twisted as the helicopter rose and tilted. "Yes!" he yelled, raising one arm while holding Vampie with the other. "This is better than the Coaster of Death at the carnival!"

Lobo's huge smile changed into a wince of pain. He felt a sting on his leg and turned to see Devon squeezing him. Her eyes were closed and her other hand was red from gripping a seat handle.

"Don't tell me you're afraid of this?"

"I've never really flown before," Devon answered.

"You can't be serious. You have wings! Don't you have to be able to fly if you want to be a guardian angel?"

"Yes," Devon answered, her eyes shut tightly. "But once I earn my flying wings, I'll control my flight and I won't be in this death trap with this loud noise. I don't think it will be anything like this... Aaah! Did you feel that? We're going to crash!"

Lobo laughed for the first time in days. "We're fine, Devon. Open your eyes. If you get used to this, then you'll be able to fly through anything."

"Okay. I'll try." Devon slowly opened one eye.

Lobo leaned forward and yelled over the loud chopper blades. "Tim, can you make this ride a little more fun?"

Tim gave Lobo a thumbs up sign and a big smile. He immediately had the chopper take a steep downward turn.

Devon snapped her eyes shut again. "I'm gonna beat you down hard with a stick. Real hard."

After twenty more minutes of flying like an amusement park ride, the helicopter steadied.

"I have to pretend I'm a regular pilot now," Tim yelled back at his passengers. "We're heading into the city. We should be there shortly."

Devon finally eased her grip on Lobo's leg. It tingled and Lobo was sure he had a bruise in the shape of Devon's fingers.

The open grassland that had been below them was soon replaced with houses and buildings.

"We're about to pass over downtown Dallas," Tim said. "It's a nice view."

The trio looked out of the window and saw skyscrapers. The chopper hovered over a few of the taller ones, then started to descend.

"Why are we going down?" Lobo asked.

"This is your destination."

"On top of a building?"

Tim nodded. As the helicopter lowered, they saw a large "X" on top of the skyscraper below them. They landed right on it.

Once the chopper's blades slowed down enough for everyone to hear each other without screaming, Lobo turned his communicator on.

"Cornelius, we're on a building."

"Yes, this is where we've narrowed the signal,"

Cornelius said. "The best place for someone to hide would be to become a regular member of society. We haven't gotten anyone near enough to the building to confirm exactly where the signal's coming from. We just know it's in one of the higher floors. The signal will be uploaded to your glasses."

"Are we just supposed to wander around and hope we're not caught?"

"This mission should be easier. There are more than one hundred different companies in this building. It has more than thirty floors. Your 'Uncle' Tim has a meeting with a bank on the twenty-eighth floor. If anyone sees you, just say you're waiting for him and are exploring. Just find out where that signal's coming from. No more communication with me once you find the right floor. You also can't risk voice communication with each other, so take a Baron Watch from your bag so Tim can let you know when he's ready."

"A Baron Watch?" Lobo asked.

Baron's voice jumped in. "It runs on radio waves and will notify you when Tim signals you. Just wrap it around your wrist like a watch. It may be primitive, but was one of my first inventions for Mr. Coronado. It's undetectable, keeps perfect time and is exactly what we need in this particular case."

"Okay," Lobo answered. "We're going."

He grabbed the bag from his pocket and said, "Baron Watch." He pulled out a small square watch with a round light in the center and slipped it on his left wrist.

Devon, Lobo and Vampie the dog followed their second fake uncle in a week inside the building and down the elevator to the twenty-eighth floor. Tim walked toward a door with a sign reading "Texas Bank Headquarters."

"I should be in here for twenty to thirty minutes," he

said. "Mr. Coronado said you should have watch signals on you. It'll make noise and blink green when I call you. Meet me here."

Lobo led them into the crowded elevator. They moved up and down a few floors and the people trickled out with each stop. On the thirtieth floor, the last passengers exited and the three were alone.

Lobo whispered. "I don't know if they have cameras, so keep quiet. The signal isn't getting clearer, it just beeps faster or slower."

"Then we'll just need to move one floor at a time if we have to," Devon said.

Lobo agreed and they continued back up each floor. The beeping starting getting faster once they hit floor thirty-three. Lobo pointed up. "We're closer."

As the elevator slowed on the thirty-sixth floor, the beeping was so fast it was almost solid. They moved up one more floor to be sure, but the beep slowed. Lobo hit number 36 again. "Looks like we found our winner."

They moved down the long hall of the floor, passing several doors. They saw offices for lawyers, computer companies and two fast food headquarters. After passing a few more doors, the signal changed to a bright blue color.

Lobo slowed his steps. "I think it's the next one." The next door was black with a large peephole in it. The sign read "Old West Home Design and Security."

"How are we going to get in?"

Devon pressed her face against one of the glass windows. "I don't think that's going to be a problem. There's a ton of people in there."

The door opened, startling the three. A family walked out raving about light fixtures and doorknobs. They didn't seem to notice the two children and their dog walk right past them.

A lone receptionist sat at her desk. She was on the phone and had two people waiting to speak with her. There were several voices in the next room. The top of the doorway said "Showroom."

The room contained different sections of home supplies. They passed sinks with gold faucets, doors, carpet samples and a section filled with different types of security cameras.

"This company provides dwelling parts?" Devon asked.

"It looks that way," Lobo answered. "They have security systems, too."

The room was full of customers.

"Business must be good," Lobo said.

Devon pointed. "Maybe not as good as it seems. Look at the couple near the door parts."

A short man and tall woman were holding different samples of wooden door frames. The man was biting on a piece of wood and then banged it against his head. The woman shrugged. The couple appeared to have no idea what the wood was for.

A man in a suit walked up to the couple. He had a gold tag on his black jacket and motioned for them to follow. He led them through a back door.

"I don't think they were human," Devon said. "Mixing with regular people is a good way to sneak in any non-humans."

They checked the rest of the customers in the showroom. Most of them looked like normal Earthlings picking and choosing ways to customize their homes, but some of them were off. A thin lady with thick calves kept feeling a stained glass window with her nose. Another man had taken his shoe off and was trying to stick his toes in a bathtub spout.

"This can work to our advantage," Devon said. "With

all of this commotion, if we follow our hyper dog to the back area, no one would suspect anything."

Vampie wagged his tail and panted as his tongue hung out.

Lobo and Devon stared at him, but Vampie just stared back.

"Apparently, our dog isn't too bright," Devon said as she gave Vampie a soft kick.

Vampie growled at her.

"If you want to keep those teeth, you'd better stick them back in your mouth, bloodsucker."

Vampie flipped around, sticking his rear up in Devon's direction.

Another couple was following a man in a black jacket. Vampie trotted behind them and stuck his body through the door, preventing it from closing. Lobo and Devon snuck through.

They walked past a hall of offices until they reached another room where another receptionist was typing on her computer keyboard. The door behind her had a large nameplate on it that read "Clint West, President."

They moved past the desk and into the next hallway, but they didn't find anyone there.

"Where are we going?" Devon asked.

"I don't know. Maybe we should just try some of the other offices."

They heard a door open further down the hall and then voices approached.

"Micah, that was quite interesting. . ."

A loud grunt cut the man off in mid-sentence.

"I meant, my, uh, congratulations to you, Mr. West," the voice continued. "You've done well for yourself. May we proceed to the document room?"

"Did he say 'Micah?'" Lobo asked, but Devon covered

his mouth as footsteps approached.

Devon pulled Lobo back and pushed him into a break room filled with soda and snack machines.

The footsteps passed and the conversation continued. "Mr. West, are these the final plans we'll be seeing, or are they still a rough draft?"

"They are final. The room is just ahead." West's voice was deep and filled the hall.

They passed by the breakroom. Lobo snuck a look and noticed the wood-eating man walk by, but didn't see West.

Devon poked his arm. "We need to get into his office."

Vampie jumped up and trotted out.

"Looks like he has an idea," Devon said.

They followed him back toward West's receptionist area, but Vampie darted out of sight. They heard a commotion and Vampie ran back toward the showroom with something dangling from his mouth.

"Hey, I need that," the receptionist yelled. She rushed after Vampie limping. One of her shoes was missing.

Lobo and Devon rushed to the office. The door was locked.

Devon reached for the keyhole. "Do I risk it?"

"No, hold on. Let's try a non-magical way first."

He pulled the lock pick out of his Baron Bag.

"Hurry, Lobo."

It didn't take long. The lock snapped open.

"So much for their security business," Lobo said.

"They may not be as concerned if they have cameras everywhere."

The room was big but looked like a regular business office with an executive desk and leather chair. The walls were filled with paintings of the Old West, including horses, saloons and cowboys. A large cabinet, bookshelf and small door completed the room.

"Check the desk," Lobo said.

They checked all the drawers, but only found some notepads and documents.

Devon threw a stack of folders down. "He's not dumb enough to leave important information in opened drawers."

Lobo moved to the large file cabinet and pulled on the top drawer. This time it was locked.

Devon inspected the cabinet. "This thing has three locks. I can get that open faster than the pick."

"Okay, just do it fast."

Devon raised her hand, but a noise outside the door startled them.

"Stupid dog," they heard the receptionist's voice say. More noise followed. "Mr. West, back so soon? I take it your meeting went well."

The knob turned, but West and his receptionist continued their conversation. Lobo darted toward the smaller door in the back with Devon right behind. Mr. West entered the room. Lobo and Devon were in a private bathroom, which was twice the size of Lobo's room at the Academy. They left the door open just enough to be able to peek in the office, leaving them a partial view of Mr. West's desk.

West sat down in his chair and picked up the desk phone.

"It's West. Any changes?" He paused. "I think I can be there tonight. Let me check."

West reached into his coat pocket and pulled out a cell phone. He tapped the screen a few times.

"No, I'm booked. It'll have to be tomorrow morning, and I expect better progress. Time is getting away from us. Do..."

A loud beeping sound echoed in the office. Lobo and

Devon jumped and closed the door.

Devon pointed at Lobo's wrist. The Baron Watch face was pulsing green and emitting a high-pitched squeal.

"Hold on. I think a fire alarm just went off," West said, getting out of his chair.

Devon got up to run, but Lobo threw a towel at her. "Wrap it around your neck and follow me."

West banged on the door. "Is someone in my bathroom?"

Lobo burst out of the room. He was holding a wash towel over the lower part of his face like a bank robber and ran straight for the front door.

"I got you, Sis," Lobo yelled as he pointed his finger back, pretending he was shooting a gun. "No cowgirl's gonna catch me."

He ran out the front door and crouched, looking back to check on Devon. She followed, but without understanding what Lobo was doing, she had put the towel around her head like a sweatband. She ran right into Mr. West, who grabbed her by the shoulders.

"What are you two doing in my office?"

"Just playing a game, I think, sir. I'm supposed to be some kind of cowgirl."

"A cowgirl?" West's face softened. "I think you have your bandana in the wrong place." West lowered the towel from Devon's head to her neck. "It's not polite to play in people's offices, young girl. You and your brother need to find your parents."

"Thank you, sir." Devon gave him a hug, then strolled out of the office.

Lobo moved through the hallway and toward the elevators where Vampie was waiting. He heard Devon's footsteps behind him as West asked his receptionist how the kids had gotten in. He was moving too fast to hear the rest. Devon reached the elevators just as the doors were opening.

Devon slapped Lobo's arm. "Thanks for making sure I got out okay."

"I was right by the door when he grabbed you, but I was afraid he'd recognize me."

"But he hasn't seen you before, has he?"

"Cornelius said he knew my father. He might have seen a resemblance. Is he following you?"

"No, he thought we were just kids playing a game, so I gave him a hug and walked out. We should still head out now."

"Why?"

Devon reached behind her and pulled up the phone.

"You got his cell phone?" Lobo started pressing the elevator down button over and over. "We gotta go."

They rushed to meet Tim and they made it back to the helicopter without anyone following them. The engine started and the blades began to spin when Devon yelled, "Something's happening."

Two security guards ran onto the roof and started waving for Tim to stay down.

"Go, Tim," Lobo said. "Go now."

The guards realized Tim wasn't going to stop and broke into a run, but the chopper was already rising. West burst through the door and rushed to the helipad. He saw Devon through the window and grabbed a gun from a guard.

West raised the weapon. "Bring that down! I need that phone, you little thief!"

Tim shifted and hit full speed. Shots rang out and metal pings hit the craft. The helicopter didn't stop and within minutes they were at a safe distance.

"That was close," Tim yelled back at his passengers. "But I think we're okay."

They were soon over fields again when the helicopter jerked hard to the left.

"What was that?" Devon said. Her hand was still on Lobo's leg, but she was doing much better on the return trip since Tim wasn't doing acrobatics.

"We may have sustained some damage. The engine's not reacting well."

The chopper sputtered a few more times.

"I'm losing control. Lobo, there's a black bag in a compartment behind you. Get it now and grab what's inside."

Lobo found the bag and pulled out several palm-sized plastic squares.

"What do I do with these?"

"Put one of them against the middle of your chest and press on it."

Lobo did as instructed and four thin strings jumped out of the square and wrapped around his torso. The square then rode down one of the lines until it circled around his back.

"Devon, you do the same," Tim yelled. "You're going to have to jump."

Devon's hands were trembling. "Jump out of this thing? Down there?"

"Those are special parachutes that Mr. Coronado gave me. They should open automatically, but right now, we're too close to the ground. I'm going to get up as high as I can. One of you will have to hold the dog."

"What about you?" Lobo said.

"I'm going to try and land her once you're all out safely. If I can't, I'll jump after you."

Lobo placed a square on Tim's chest. The helicopter started turning in circles as they ascended.

"You have to go now," Tim said.

Lobo pulled the door open. "Go, Devon."

"I can't do this, Lobo. What if these don't work?"

Lobo looked at Devon's plastic square. "It has Baron's name on it. I'd trust him."

"I can't move!"

Lobo placed his hand on Devon's shoulder. "Remember when you threw me in the pool?"

Devon nodded.

"Well, consider this payback."

He shoved her out of the helicopter and she screeched on her way out, then he grabbed Vampie and jumped.

The ground rushed toward them. Although the chopper had risen higher, they still seemed too low for a skydive.

Lobo felt something snap on his back and his fall started to slow. He looked down at Devon and saw two wings dart out of the square. Two yellow strings then shot out and wrapped around her ankles. The strings spun and formed plastic looking triangles that hugged the wind. Lobo's legs jerked and he saw the same mini-sails on his own ankles.

They were gliding.

They moved downward in big circles. The helicopter buzzed by, heading straight down. Tim jumped out just before the chopper crashed and exploded. His glider deployed a few seconds before he hit the ground and he drifted near the fireball.

Devon and Lobo landed on their feet and their gliders retracted back into their plastic squares. They rushed toward the crash site.

Lobo stopped. "I don't see him."

"There," Devon pointed.

Tim was near a large tree, face down. Lobo reached him and turned him on his back.

"Is he alive?" Devon asked.

Tim answered with a groan. His face and arms were bleeding. Devon's wings glowed as she put her hands on his chest and tried to heal him.

"He'll live, but he has too many injuries. I can't fix them all."

Lobo flipped his communicator back on and informed his grandfather.

"I won't get to you in time," Cornelius said. "A helicopter on fire attracts attention. You need to get out of there."

"We can't leave Tim here," Lobo said.

Tim grabbed Lobo's arm. "I can't let you get caught. Whatever Devon did, I feel better. Now leave before the authorities show up. I'll be fine."

The three ran down the field. They heard cars and sirens but were far enough from the road that they wouldn't be noticed. They neared several farm houses. The occupants were outside, trying to get a better look at the burning helicopter.

Lobo tugged Devon's arm. "That lady's holding a sleeping baby."

A woman had her napping child over her shoulder.

"Do we wait for her to put the baby down?" Devon asked.

"No," Lobo said. "We need to get out of here now. I'm sure they're looking for us."

They walked around the back of the house and approached the woman from behind.

"Excuse me?" Lobo said, startling the woman. "Can you help us?"

"Where did you children come from?" the lady asked.

Lobo opened his mouth, but couldn't think of anything to say.

"We were in that helicopter," Devon said. "We died in

the crash. We'll probably haunt this place for a few years."

The woman gasped as Devon reached for the baby's head and the three vanished before her eyes.

CHAPTER FIFTEEN: EXAMINATION

They exited next to a baby sleeping in a playpen and escaped through a back door.

"That woman's going to have nightmares the rest of her life," Lobo said.

"You panicked and so did I. You humans are resilient. I'm sure she'll be okay."

"True," Lobo replied. "Maybe she'll be able to sleep after a few years of therapy."

It took them almost twenty minutes to reach the training compound by foot. Cornelius cruised into the room.

"How did you get here?" he asked. "There's not a portal within miles of your location."

Lobo turned to Devon, but she looked down and didn't answer.

"I'm not sure," Lobo said. "I thought you had zapped us out of there somehow."

Devon couldn't hide her smile.

"I'll leave it alone for now, but I expect there was magic

involved. What did you find?"

Lobo explained what had happened and how he was sure Mr. West was really Dukane.

"You didn't get anything solid?" Cornelius asked.

"No, I didn't. But Devon has something."

Lobo held out the cell phone.

"Excellent work, all of you. I'll have Baron go through this immediately."

"If you don't mind, Grandfather, I'd like to look over Baron's shoulder."

"Why, Jeremiah? It may be way above your head."

"You said my father was a great detective. I want to know if he gave any of that to me."

"It can't be any worse than your combat skills," Devon snorted.

Lobo tried to stare her down, but couldn't help smiling. "She's right. I'm hoping I'm better at being a detective than I am at fighting."

"That's fine, Jeremiah," Cornelius said. "Maybe Devon and Vampie would like to join you."

"No, thanks," Devon replied. "I'd rather practice fighting some more."

Vampie had already transformed. "I'll join you, Lobo. I still need to do my job."

"Oh," Lobo said. "Can you get some blood for Vampie? He had a horse snack at the ranch, but he needs something a little more regular."

"Of course."

"Nothing human," Vampie said.

"Too bad," Cornelius replied. "I have plenty of that in the back."

The three looked at him, surprised. Cornelius half-smiled and left them wondering whether he was joking or not.

Lobo and Vampie returned to Baron's workshop, where he led them toward a back room.

Baron hooked the cell phone up to a machine that projected its contents onto the table where they were seated. Vampie stood in the background taking notes.

The table listed different document names, but they weren't in English. "These files are encrypted," Baron said. "But they won't be for long."

He attached a black box to the phone and each letter in the file names started blinking. Within thirty seconds, the names were all in English.

"There," Baron said. "All decrypted."

There were multiple files listed in alphabetical order. Baron touched a file name on the table and it expanded. Lobo repeated the process until the table was covered with full pages.

"Here," Lobo said. "This one says something about the Zaan."

He and Baron read through it.

"Alina said the Zaan is a ceremony meant to take over the world," Lobo said. "But there was a chain of events that led to it. Are these the steps?"

"Yes," Baron answered. "There are four. The first is a simple incantation that starts the process. The second involves a relic called the Time Dial of the Zaan. It's a celestial clock that counts down forty days to complete the ceremony. These first two events have already occurred. The clock is ticking. The third step is activating the alignment of the six demon realms. The alignment will take between twenty to forty hours, depending on the time of year. Once the alignment is complete, the final ceremony must be held on a demon realm. If successful, this will give the Summoner enough power to rule the Earth."

"Who is the Summoner?" Lobo asked.

"The one that begins the final ceremony. The one who desires this ultimate power."

Baron scanned the rest of the file. "This document doesn't really help us. We need to find out details on the final ceremony."

They continued browsing.

"Look at this one," Lobo said. "The one called 'Earp.'" The file name's been decrypted, but the page doesn't make sense. What do all those symbols mean?"

The page contained multiple squiggles, dots and lines and only a few of them repeated. Some were as simple as squares and wavy lines, while others were complex shapes that Lobo didn't recognize.

"If my decrypter didn't pick it up, then it has to be using a key code."

"What's a key code?"

"Most decryption programs resolve to a language character, so a junk symbol or decryption would stand for the letter 'M'. That's how the other files were decrypted. Here, these symbols stand for full words or phrases, so that one wavy line may mean 'meet me at Baron's Amusement Park.'"

"You have an amusement park?"

"No," Baron sighed. "Just a wishful dream."

"So how do you figure out what they stand for?"

"You would need a key telling you exactly what each symbol represents."

"If these pages are harder to unlock than the rest, does that mean they're more important?"

"No way of knowing. They were important enough to be decrypted this way. We can't do anything with these now. Let's just focus on what we can read."

They went through more of the pages. They found three others with the same symbol decryption. Baron set them aside as he went through the unlocked documents more closely.

Baron focused on one decrypted document for a long while.

Lobo took a glance. "That looks like a shopping list."

"This could be a list for the final Zaan ceremony," Baron answered. "There are eighteen objects here. The Time Dial is the first one, but I'm not sure about some of the rest."

Lobo pulled up a copy on his side of the table. The pieces ranged from a pure two carat diamond to the tongue of a Komodo dragon. The last two items were underlined.

"What are those?" Lobo asked.

"The first item is a Gorhhad hide. That is an animal found in most of the demon realms. It has rows of sharp teeth and a spiked tail that can split most creatures in half with one swipe. Ironically, it doesn't eat meat. I don't know about the other."

Baron hit a switch near the table. "Cornelius, I need you to help me identify something."

"I'll be right there," Cornelius answered.

He showed up a moment later. "What have you found?"

"We were able to fully decrypt all but four documents," Baron explained. "We've gone through the rest, and this one could detail the final ceremony. It lists some of the items related to the Zaan, but the rest don't all fit. I can identify all but the last object. Have you ever heard of the Dreaming Soul?"

"No, I don't know what that is. Dukane probably has many plans to strengthen his position of power and these items could be a list for several of them. Objects like the Time Dial can be used for different objectives. He probably based his choice on which artifacts he could actually obtain."

"What about the documents Baron couldn't totally decrypt?" Lobo asked.

"The only thing we're certain of is the Zaan has begun. Nothing has proven otherwise. We need to concentrate on that and assume those files reference other plans that have already failed or were never started."

Cornelius's chair started beeping.

"Alina," Cornelius said. "How can I help you?"

"It's happening," Alina answered over a speaker.

"I'm here with Jeremiah. Let me put you on screen."

Cornelius hit some buttons and Alina's image appeared at the center of Baron's table.

"Good to see you again, Lobo," Alina said. "Thanks to the information your team helped us gather, we know the alignment of the demon realms is in progress and expect the ceremony to take place in the next twelve hours. The only thing we don't know is the location. Cornelius, do you have an update?"

"We determined for certain Micah Dukane is responsible," Cornelius said. "Devon obtained his personal cell phone. We're still going through his records, but it does seem the Zaan is his ultimate goal."

Baron hadn't looked up. He was still going through a few items. "Here," he said. "I think I might have found a way to link some of these documents. I'll need to run a more detailed analysis, but I should have something within a few hours."

"Excellent," Alina said. "I'll leave you to your work. Let me know as soon as you can." Her image disappeared.

Baron pressed something, then relaxed and drank a liquid that smelled like a dead rat and was emitting a green mist.

"Now what?" Lobo asked.

"I've kicked off the analysis. At this point, we wait and monitor San Francisco and the realms for unusual activity."

Lobo turned to Vampie, who was still taking notes. "Can you please leave us alone for a few minutes?"

The Scribe nodded and walked out.

"Any chance my father would know anything?" Lobo asked.

Cornelius paused. "It's possible, but I don't see the point."

"I want to talk to him again."

"Why now? We're on the verge of finding Dukane."

"I'll just be sitting here, anyway. Maybe he knows something about those files we couldn't read."

"You should wait here, Jeremiah. I can't go with you."

"I don't need an escort. Baron, can you give me these files on another phone?"

"Yes, but I'll give you more than a phone. My device can hold every book ever written on any world. It can also learn to read any form of media, even those stored in the minds of the telepaths of Dierna. I call it the Ultimate Brain."

Baron slithered toward the back of his shop and came back with the device that looked like a regular cell phone except for the casing, which looked like green Jell-O.

"Here, Lobo. I've downloaded all of Dukane's documents. Also, don't worry about the screen. It's unbreakable flex glass."

"Cool," Lobo said as he turned to his grandfather. "Can your driver take me?"

"I know better than to try and change the mind of a Coronado once he's set it. I'll notify Dr. Jansen you're on your way. I'll contact you if we find anything."

"Thank you, Grandfather."

"You'll need this." Cornelius handed Lobo the flashlight with the green beam. "The keypad code is 71937. Don't forget it."

Lobo rushed out of the room and found Devon beating down a Barna. Vampie was watching and writing. Lobo guessed he was jotting down his thoughts on Devon's anger issues.

Lobo tried to sneak by them.

"Where you off to now, Lobo?" Devon asked.

He looked down.

"Not a problem. Another 'can't trust us' moment, I take it? It's not like we've proven ourselves to each other more than a few times."

Lobo continued walking, but stopped just before walking out the door and turned back. "You're right, Devon. I'll tell you both where I'm going."

A loud noise came from the back of the room.

"Jeremiah," Cornelius said as he hovered into the room. "Remember what we discussed."

"They've earned my trust, Grandfather, and I've earned theirs."

"You're endangering. . ."

"No, I'm not. I'm going to tell them and I don't care what you say."

Cornelius' metal hand banged against his chair. "Fine. You understand your actions, then. The responsibility is yours."

He hovered out.

"Are you sure, Lobo?" Devon asked.

"My father's alive," he blurted. "I found out that day I left."

"The Grey Wolf's alive?" Vampie asked. "How?"

"My grandfather saved him but kept him hidden for his own protection since he wasn't sure who was responsible.

It turns out it was Micah Dukane. He's the one who killed my mother and tried to kill my father."

Devon put her hand on his shoulder. "I'm happy for you."

For the first time since they met, Devon looked sincere.

"I saw him at the hospital. He's sick, but he's alive. I'm going to see him again and I'd like both of you to come with me."

Vampie wrote furiously as his quills shook with excitement.

CHAPTER SIXTEEN: DETECTIVE

Lobo led his companions to the morgue and entered the keypad code to continue through the hospital. He used the green beam to get through the hidden closet door and then reached the secret room.

Dr. Jansen was waiting again. He frowned as he saw Lobo's guests. "Who is this young lady? And we don't allow dogs in here."

"It's okay. They're my friends. I'd like them to come in with me."

"I don't think that's such a good idea."

"Please, Doctor. Just this one time."

The doctor unlocked the door. "Just be sure none of you get too close. The only reason I'm agreeing to this is because I had new restraints installed and I'm confident he can't break them."

They entered and found Sebastian Coronado on his back, face turned to the wall.

"Father," Lobo said. "It's Lobo. I'm here with some friends."

Sebastian Coronado was still. Lobo walked next to the bed.

"I have new information on Dukane and I need your help. We think he's trying to complete a ceremony called the Zaan. Cornelius and Alina think this might happen in the next few hours."

Sebastian turned around. His metal restraints clanged as he turned to his son.

"There's a problem, though," Lobo continued. "We found a bunch of Dukane's files and were able to decrypt all of them except for four pages. Everyone thinks they don't mean anything, but I can't help feeling they're more important than we think."

His father stared back at him but didn't speak.

Lobo took out Baron's Ultimate Brain. He called up the file names and turned the screen toward his father.

"These are the files. They're called 'Jesse,' 'Annie,' 'Wyatt' and 'William'. They're full of all kinds of symbols that need a code key to read. Do you know anything about them?"

Sebastian stared at the screen, then sat up and turned toward his son.

"Knife," he mumbled.

"I couldn't hear you, Father. What did you say?"

"Knife. Need a blade."

Lobo pulled the supply bag out of his pocket.

"Lobo, what are you doing?" Devon asked as she stepped toward him.

Lobo waved her back. "Don't." He pulled the bag up to his mouth and whispered, "Knife." He reached in, pulled out a hunting knife and handed it to his father.

Sebastian grabbed the weapon and tried to raise his hand, but the restraint held.

Lobo looked toward the door. "Dr. Jansen, I need you

to let him go."

Dr. Jansen hit the intercom button. "That's not going to happen, Lobo. He's too dangerous."

"He's my father, Doctor. Can you at least loosen his right hand?"

"His restraints are wired. I'll be able to send electricity through him if he gets out of control, but if you're touching him, you could be injured."

"Please unlock his arm. If I think I'm in danger, I'll yell and you can shock him"

"I'm sorry, Lobo. As his doctor, I can't put you or your guests at risk."

"Devon, Vampie, please step outside," Lobo asked.

Devon stepped forward and crossed her arms. "I'm supposed to protect you."

"This is bigger than me. Please."

Devon and Vampie left the room as Dr. Jansen entered.

"It's just me now, Doctor. I'll call my grandfather if I have to."

"I'm doing this under protest," Dr. Jansen said. "I'll be watching closely." He walked back out and hit some buttons on the door panel. The restraint on Sebastian's right wrist hissed as it unlocked. Sebastian gazed at the knife in his hand. He snapped his wrist and plunged the blade into his collarbone, splattering blood over Lobo's face.

"Father, what are you doing?" Lobo pulled his father's arm back and the knife came out. Sebastian grabbed Lobo with his restrained hand.

"I'm administering the shock," Dr. Jansen screamed through the intercom.

"No," Lobo said. "Just wait."

Sebastian stuck his face within an inch of his son's. "Trust."

"I trust you, Father."

Sebastian let go of his son and then eased the knife back into his collarbone. He twisted the blade and grunted in pain as blood trickled down his chest. Something popped. Sebastian pointed the knife low and scooped it upwards. A small white bone was protruding from his wound. He handed Lobo the knife, then reached into his cut with two fingers and pulled out the exposed bone. He held it out and handed it to his son.

Dr. Jansen rushed in. "I have to bandage that wound."

Sebastian raised his hand. "Wait."

The doctor hesitated. "I'll give you five minutes," he said as he walked back out.

Lobo took the bone and examined it. It started to emit a blue light, and then he heard something beep. Baron's Ultimate Brain, which had fallen to the floor during the confusion, was flashing with activity. Lobo picked it up and the screen read, "Found Media. Awaiting Download."

Lobo moved the bone near the Brain but didn't know what to do next. He passed it in front of the screen, and the Brain started whizzing, then read, "Uploading Media Content" and within a few seconds, it read "Upload Complete." The Brain had several new file folders, one of which was titled "Dukane."

Lobo opened the folder.

"Father, there are hundreds of files in here. It'll take hours, maybe days to read them all."

"Fascinated with history. Indians, Old West, Romans. . ."

"Old West?" Lobo said. "The name of his company is Old West Home Design and Security."

Sebastian tapped the screen with a bloody finger. He was pointing to the file called "Earp."

Lobo's eyes widened. "Wyatt Earp. I remember reading

about him. He was the famous lawman from the OK Corral shootout."

Lobo opened the "Earp" file and saw a page of familiar symbols with individual words or phrases next to them. They matched the "Wyatt" document. "This is it. The key's here. I just need to match the other file names. Thank you. I need to go. I need to get these files decoded."

Sebastian put his hand on his son's shoulder. "Careful who you trust."

"I will."

"Not even me. Head broken."

"I understand. I know what he did to Mother and to you. I'm going to finish this."

"Channel fear," Sebastian said as his face twitched. "Channel anger. Powerful allies."

Lobo let the words sink in and he embraced his father. "Thank you. I'll come back and see you soon."

Dr. Jansen came back in and started working on Sebastian's wound as Lobo walked out. The three rushed to the car and headed back to the training facility.

Lobo sat in the back seat, staring at the Ultimate Brain.

"Are you going to tell Cornelius about this?" Devon asked.

"Only if we find anything. Baron said this Brain could hold every book ever written. I need to figure out how to work this fast."

Lobo used the touch screen and noticed a "Find" feature. He hit it, and the Brain spoke, startling them all. "State search item, please," a soothing voice said.

Lobo held the Brain near his mouth like a microphone. "The Old West."

A long list of titles came up, but there were too many. A button blinked on top that read "Advanced Search." Lobo touched it and more options appeared. He hit "Data

Find." The Brain spoke. "Please state search data."

"Names of famous characters from the Old West."

"Fiction or non-fiction?" the voice asked.

"Non-Fiction."

A shorter list of names appeared. "I think Jesse refers to Jesse James," Lobo explained to his friends. "He was a famous gunfighter."

Lobo flipped back toward Dukane's list and found "James." He pulled up the symbols and compared them to the "Jesse" file. "They match. Let's check Annie now."

He went down the list and found Annie Oakley. He selected her name. "This says she was famous for being a good shooter."

He found the matching "Oakley" file.

"All that's left is William." He went down the list. "There's no William here."

"Just decode the three you know and we can worry about that one later," Devon said. "We're almost at the training center."

"You're right, we shouldn't waste any time. It would be easier if I could print these out. The screen isn't so big."

"Name of file to print?" the Brain asked.

Lobo flipped the Brain around and studied it. "How is this going to print?"

"File name not found," the Brain replied.

"Baron's supposed to be a genius," Devon said.

"Print 'Annie,' 'Oakley,' 'Jesse,' 'James,' 'Wyatt,' 'Earp' and 'William,'" Lobo instructed.

The Brain clicked a few times and one side snapped and started to lengthen. Sheets of paper started emerging from the longer side.

"Impressive," Vampie said. "That's much faster than my quills."

Once the printing completed, Lobo placed the related

files side by side. "It'll be faster if we do this together."

"You trust us with this?" Devon asked.

Lobo smiled. "Without a doubt."

Lobo took Wyatt Earp, Devon took Jesse James and Vampie took Annie Oakley. They started copying the words and phrases from the key onto the coded pages. The car stopped.

"We're here," Devon said.

They entered the training facility, but no one greeted them. Lobo flipped on his communicator. "Cornelius, we've returned."

"Busy, Jeremiah. We've eliminated three demon realms and are close to finding the location of the ceremony. Anything from your father?"

"Maybe. We're still researching. We're going to find a room and go over our stuff."

"Very well," Cornelius said.

They found an open door near Baron's workshop. There was a long table and some chairs. Lobo put his documents on the table. "Perfect. Let's finish these here."

They set up and continued. Twenty minutes later, Vampie put his quills down. "I'm finished, but not all of the symbols are complete."

Devon slapped her hands down. She was less than halfway done. "Those Finger Quills give you too much of an advantage. Get over here and help us."

Vampie stood on his seat and took turns translating Lobo and Devon's documents. Soon, all three were complete, but some symbols remained unknown.

"What are we missing?" Devon asked. "Each page has symbols that aren't in the key."

Lobo glanced over the documents. "Here. Check out Wyatt Earp and Annie Oakley. Annie Oakley finishes what Wyatt Earp started and also has another symbol key."

They looked at the combined Wyatt Earp document, which read:

> The following ritual must be performed on the soil of the realm ₪. In order, the following items must be pierced through the ∞ when the third moon of ₪, burns brightest:
>
> ∂
> ╪
> ≡

The Annie Oakley document read:

> Once completed, a level 2 demon must be sacrificed on the ∞, providing the ultimate weapon of fire.
>
> ∂ - Serpent tail
> ╪ - Korindian snout
> ∞ - Horn of a Morta
> ≡ - Tongue of a Demon Traitor
> ₪ - Torakan

Lobo filled in the missing symbols, completing the document.

> The following ritual must be performed on the soil of the realm Torakan.
>
> In order, the following items must be pierced through the Horn of a Morta when the third moon of Torakan burns brightest:
>
> Serpent tail
> Korindian snout
> Tongue of a Demon Traitor
>
> Once completed, a level 2 demon must be sacrificed on the Horn of a Morta, providing the ultimate weapon of fire.

"Could this be what Dukane's trying to do?" Lobo asked. "How powerful would this fire weapon be?"

"It would generate enough fire to burn entire cities with one strike, but I don't think this is it," Devon said. "The Morta have been extinct for about a thousand years."

"Could one be cloned?"

"Possibly, but the other problem's bigger. The third moon of Torakan is Kamora. It burns brightest every two hundred years when it's closest to the realm. The Torakans have a huge, disgusting celebration that lasts for days. I remember because it happened about three years ago and the celestial realms were put on high alert. So I think we're good for a while."

"Then it must be the other files. Jesse James must match up with William and the missing doc. Look at Jesse James. Does it make any sense to you?"

Jesse James contents:

Demon King:

δ unspoiled by human hands must be used on the Φ to find the Ω. The final Ritual must occur on a heavenly realm. Ψ must be mixed in the ⏁. The human subject must drink the mix, then spill the combined Ψ.

"This means nothing," Devon said. "They have to drink something. Could be lizard juice, for all we know."

"Then we need to figure out what 'William' belongs to." Lobo pulled out his Ultimate Brain and tried the list again. "None of these characters are named William."

"Could there be another name?" Vampie asked.

"What do you mean?"

"In my records, I'm documenting all that we've been through. When I describe you, I must refer to you by your proper birth name, Jeremiah. However, when I chronicle someone's speech, it's usually just Lobo. Two names, same person."

"You mean a nickname? I hadn't even thought about it. The nickname for William is Bill."

"Bill?" Devon asked. "Why isn't it Will?"

"It could be Will, or Willy, or Billy, I suppose. I didn't make up the nickname rules, but I've always heard Bill. I'll check them all."

Lobo scanned through the list. There were no Will's, but two Bill's pulled up. Wild Bill Hickok and Billy the Kid. Lobo flipped to the list of Dukane's files. No "Wild," "Hickok," or "Kid."

"Nothing," he said. "Maybe the books will give me more information."

Lobo read through Wild Bill Hickok's file. Wild Bill was

a lawman and a gambler, but nothing stood out that matched any file names.

He tried Billy the Kid's file. The first line stated, "Billy the Kid was surrounded in mystery and legend. His birth name was Patrick Henry McCarty. He had several aliases, including William H. Bonney, Henry Antrim and the Kid."

Lobo searched. He didn't find a matching Patrick or Henry.

"Bonney," Lobo said as the name came up. "It's William Bonney." Lobo clicked it open. "This is it."

The three rushed to decrypt the "William" file. It read:

> This will summon the Ж, which must be given the essence of the Ω. If the subject is worthy, the Ж will give him the power to rule the six dark realms.
>
> Key Items:
> δ - Golden Ore
> Ψ - Demon Blood from each Realm
> ⋺ - Human King's Chalice
> Ж - Anointer
> Φ - Eye of the Traveler
> Ω - Dreaming Soul

"Let's finish it." He jotted in the missing symbols. The completed document read:

Demon King:
Golden Ore unspoiled by human hands must be used on the Eye of the Traveler to find the Dreaming Soul. The final Ritual must occur on a heavenly realm. Demon Blood from each Realm must be mixed in the Human King's Chalice. The human subject must drink the mix, then spill the combined Demon Blood from each Realm.

This will summon the Anointer, which must be given the essence of the Dreaming Soul. If the subject is worthy, the Anointer will give him the power to rule the six dark realms.

"This mentions the Dreaming Soul and the Eye of the Traveler," Lobo said. "Those were also on the list for the Zaan. What if the Zaan is just a big distraction and this is what he's really planning? Does this Demon King ritual seem possible, Devon?"

Devon didn't give a quick answer. She scanned the page several times. "It could be."

"How do we find out for sure?"

"Golden ore is only found on Earth, and so is the King's Chalice."

"Gold can be found all over the world," Lobo said. "Wait, the Old West. There was a Gold Rush during that time in California."

"Is it possible there's still some there?"

"They couldn't have found it all. Plus, it would have to be ore that was never touched by a human before. That could explain the mine we saw in San Francisco."

"That's promising, but nothing solid," Devon said. "What about the King's Chalice?"

"Something like that would probably be in a museum somewhere. We can find out if any are missing."

"We don't have time to travel to all the museums on your planet."

"We just need a computer to search the internet."

The room contained two computers. Lobo moved to one of the keyboards and did a search on "Stolen Chalice" and got several hits. Some were several years old, but one was recent.

"This article says that a museum in Spain was robbed last month. They took gold artifacts, and one of them was a chalice belonging to King Ferdinand of Spain.

"We're getting closer," Devon said. "Lobo, use the Brain to pull up any information on the Eye of the Traveler. I've read a little about it. It's supposed to help you find any object on any world."

Lobo searched the Ultimate Brain and chose the first document it found. He read part of it aloud. "The Eye of the Traveler can be mixed with various items, each dependent on what is being searched for. Once in place, one must simply ask for what they seek. The only limitation is that once a stimulating item is placed on the Eye, the Eye must remain in the same spot with the item intact until the object being searched for is recovered."

"That means the ore needs to stay on the Eye until the Dreaming Soul is found," Devon said. "If the Eye is where the ore is. . ."

"There's only one way to know for sure," Lobo said. "We have to go back to San Francisco."

CHAPTER SEVENTEEN: WORKAROUND

"Let's go," Devon said. "I don't think we're near any sleeping babies. We need to go through the portal."

They rushed toward the pool. Lobo reached the bottom first but didn't see a glow. He jammed his foot into where the portal should be, but nothing happened. Devon followed behind but wasn't able to get through, either. As Lobo stuck his head out of the water, he heard Cornelius's voice over the intercom. "Why are you trying the portal, Jeremiah?"

"I'm following up on a lead."

"All non-authorized portal travel has been halted until we find the location of the ceremony."

"We need to go now, Cornelius," Lobo pleaded.

"You risk opening the portal for Dukane. No exceptions." The intercom squeaked off.

Lobo turned to his companions. "There has to be another way. Let's talk to Baron."

They rushed to Baron's workshop and found him working on more of Dukane's files.

"Baron," Lobo said. "We need your help. Portal travel's been stopped, but we need to get back to San Francisco."

"You've found something?" Baron asked.

"We're not sure. It could be nothing, or it could be everything. We just need to get there now."

"I do have an alternative, but it's untested."

"What?"

"It's a travel vehicle. It's made up of parts from many worlds. If it works, you can be in San Francisco within two minutes."

"What are the risks?" Vampie asked.

"The risk is to humans and possibly you, Vampire. Cherubs should be okay. This vehicle is meant to be fast, but the speed would pull the skin right off Lobo's face. It doesn't work for most creatures, which is why I had scrapped the idea in the first place."

"Then it's not an option," Devon said.

"If you can use your Cherub skills to put a protective shield around your companions, they should be safe."

"Should?"

"Like I stated, it hasn't been tested. I have many safety measures installed. We could start at a slower speed just to make sure Lobo's skin stays on."

Lobo's face went pale. "That would be nice."

Baron's tail slapped against the floor. "Plus, I would be delighted to know if it actually works. Come." He led them into another room behind his workshop that was half the size of the training area. Baron pulled out a small remote and hit a few buttons. The ground opened and a cigar shaped ship emerged. It was wide, but only a few inches longer than Lobo's body.

"How are we going to fit in that?" Lobo asked.

"I have a compression chamber inside. It will shrink your bodies to fit. You won't notice it."

Devon started toward the vehicle.

"Wait," Lobo said. "They sealed the entrance from Alcatraz. How are we going to get in this time?"

"I wasn't sure if anyone was going to have to return," Baron answered. "However, we've continued monitoring since your first mission. There is another way in. The energy used inside requires a larger amount of power and generates heat, which needs a way to cool off. Exhaust is released every few minutes into the bay to handle this. There are panel openings that should be large enough for all of you to get through."

"I can't swim," Lobo said. "How do we get underwater?"

"The vehicle is amphibious."

The three looked back at him with blank stares.

"Meaning that besides flying, it also works on land and water. You'll move so fast they shouldn't be able to detect you since nothing like this exists."

"This is the only option we have right now, so we have to try," Lobo said. "We'll start slow, right? I want my face in the same place when we land."

"Yes, all of you get in."

A small hatch opened on the side of the cylinder. Only Vampie looked like he would be able to fit.

"Don't be shy, just step in. The compression will work on contact at the cellular level."

Devon took the first step and her foot shrunk as she inserted it into the vehicle. "Feels funky."

She stuck her entire body in. Lobo closed his eyes and got in as well. Vampie followed. The three were stuck together as they tried to get comfortable, but once they settled in they had some wiggle room between them. The hatch closed.

Baron's voice filled the capsule. "Be ready. I'm opening

the roof."

Lobo looked through a thin window around the upper part of the vehicle. He saw Baron hit another button and then looked up as a panel on the roof opened.

"If anything happens, just yell," Baron said. "I'll be able to hear you. Devon, start the protection field."

Devon closed her eyes and the protective bubble enclosed them. "It's done. We're ready."

"Baron," Lobo asked. "What do you call this thing?"

"It depends on how this goes. If it works, I'll call it the Supershot. If it doesn't, probably the Pancake Maker."

Baron's finger came down on the remote and then a streak of light followed as the vehicle moved faster than anything on Earth.

"Is everyone alive?" Baron's voice asked a moment later.

Even with the bubble, the three cramped companions were shaking with the pressure.

"We're okay right now," Devon yelled.

"I'm taking it faster." The pressure increased and the shaking grew worse.

"You're about thirty seconds from hitting San Francisco Bay. I'm calculating a safe landing spot. I wouldn't want you crashing into any boats."

Vampie passed out.

"Just a few more seconds. Keep that shield strong, Devon. You're going to decrease speed almost as fast as you increased it. Here we go. 3-2-1..."

They hit the water hard and Lobo's head jerked back.

"You can drop the bubble now, Devon."

Lobo shook Vampie awake. From the window, he saw a school of fish swim by.

Devon used her superior eyesight to look ahead. "I see the tube from Alcatraz."

A few seconds later, Lobo and Vampie saw it, too. As they neared the location, a large burst of bubbles shot out from where the tube connected to land.

"That's got to be it," Lobo said.

Baron's voice echoed in the ship. "It appears that my Supershot was a success. Now, you need to get into that exhaust system. Once you're a little closer, the external cameras on the Supershot will give me better measurements."

They moved closer to the exhaust, which let out another round of bubbles.

"The opening's not large enough for the vehicle," Baron said. "You'll have to swim through."

"Two problems," Lobo said. "First, as hard as I tried, I still didn't learn how to swim in the last five minutes. Second, if the exhaust is shooting pressure out, how are we going to get through?"

"The first one's easy," Baron replied. "There are some oxygen mouthpieces in the small blue panel that will allow you to breathe. They contain material like your ear communicators that will conform to your nasal cavities so you don't get water up your noses. If you have any issues, I'm sure Devon or Vampie can pull you along."

"How about getting inside?"

"That's going to be trickier. I think the best thing to do would be to shoot a retracting line through the vents once they open. If it attaches to a solid surface, it can pull you through the pressure. Based on the last few readings, it looks like you'll have about ten seconds to make it."

"How is it going to pull us?" Lobo asked.

"It's my own design. The cable is tough enough to support five elephants, but the metal is a porous interlocking material that can be shifted any way, even multiple directions at the same time. The cable is infested with tiny vermin from the demon worlds that are attracted to electric pulses, which allows me to control movement."

Devon stuck her tongue out. "So, we're going to be touching tiny demon bugs?"

"Yes, plus you'll have to eat them after or they'll consume your flesh."

The trio stared at each other in horror.

"Hello?" Baron asked as he tapped his communicator. "Is this on? Do they not have sarcasm on Osidian?"

They all let out their breath.

"You will need to get into position and let me know when you're ready. The window's going to be small. Once you're all through the vent, you still need enough time for the line to get in behind you."

Devon shook her head. "Why can't you just shoot the line through and leave it? If the cable's as strong as you say it is, it probably won't break when the vent's closed."

"That's not the problem. If it does not close properly, it could damage the vent and set off an alarm. We need to fire the line, shoot the three of you and the line through within the ten-second gap."

Devon nodded. "I can hold Vampie, so you'll only need to pull Lobo and me through."

"Even better. Get your mouthpieces on. You'll be able to communicate with them. I'll flood the Supershot shortly and then open the hatch and you can get in position. We need to get within one hundred feet of the vents to make the ten-second window."

The ship moved closer as Lobo found the mouthpieces in the blue panel. He handed a set to his teammates.

"I think we're ready, Baron," Lobo said.

He grimaced as the nose plugs expanded into his nostrils. "I'm a little nervous."

"I'll keep you from drowning, Lobo," Devon said.

Lobo managed a weak smile. "I know you will, Dev."

"We've reached the distance," Baron said. "I'm opening the Supershot now."

The hatch opened and water filled the ship. Lobo's insides were twisting, but he kept his composure as Devon and then Vampie swam out, leaving him alone. Lobo gripped the sides of the hatch and floated out, but didn't let go of the Supershot.

Devon grabbed his arm. "It's okay, Lobo. I've got you."

Lobo stared at his fingers and watched each digit rise until he was free.

"The vents will have just enough room to pull you through," Baron explained. "Make sure that you are right behind one another and not side by side or you might get smashed into pieces."

The tip of the Supershot split open and a flashlight shaped piece of metal with a pointy edge emerged.

"I'm going to let out two small strands from the back of the cable launcher. Clasp your hands around them and the demon mites will wrap around your grip."

Devon placed a hand on one of the loose strands and a swarm that looked like electric ants covering a bitten apple devoured her up to her wrist. "This is disgusting."

"Don't let go," Baron warned. "If you try and grab the cable with your bare hands, the speed and force will most likely rip your fingers and bones apart."

With Devon still holding his arm, Lobo placed his hands on the second strand and let the mites do their work. They held him firmly, but the grip was gentle enough to make him feel as if he could break free if he had to. Devon let Lobo go but kept him in sight.

"I'm okay," Lobo said. "Get Vampie ready and secure your other hand."

Vampie wrapped his thin limbs around Devon's back.

Devon clasped her hands together. "We're ready, Baron."

"The vents should open in about fifteen seconds. It's going to fire fast, so just hold your breath. You'll feel the pressure, but I guarantee you that your hands will still be attached."

Vampie tucked his head deep into Devon's torso. Lobo noticed she was breathing faster, but she didn't look nervous.

"Everyone inhale," Baron said. "Here we go!"

The line shot just as a burst of bubbles flew out of the vent. Devon and Lobo saw the line take off with their hands still attached, but the rest of their bodies hadn't moved. Their arms stretched like long rubber bands as the demon mites spread over them.

In an instant, they were flung across the water, catching up to the cable strands. The tip of the cable zipped through the open vent and hit a solid chunk of soil and rock. Two seconds later, Devon and Vampie slammed through the open vent with Lobo right behind. Their bodies stopped as fast as they had taken off. The cable retracted just before the vent closed.

"We made it," Lobo said, but Baron didn't respond.

Lobo tried to speak to Devon through the mouthpiece but just heard static. They were facing each other, but he couldn't move. He knew she couldn't help him up while holding Vampie, so he pointed upward. Devon nodded then shot up. Lobo saw her feet and then nothing. He waited a few more seconds and felt himself start falling. He grabbed a big rock sticking out of the soil and held himself up.

"Devon," he said over the static. "If you can hear me, I'm kinda terrified right now and it would be a good time to come get me."

No response.

Finally, he felt hands grab him by the shoulders and pull him up.

Their heads emerged and Lobo took in a big breath. He slapped the water, splashing Devon in the face. "Thanks for the help."

"Sorry, I got distracted."

"She forgot about you," Vampie said. "I reminded her."

"Quiet," she whispered. "I'm not sure if anyone can hear us."

They pulled themselves out of the water. There wasn't a creature in sight.

The area around them looked like a huge cave. There were four large tunnel holes in front of them.

"Which one?" Lobo asked.

Devon walked a few feet into each tunnel and took a few deep whiffs. "It's the third one. It has the freshest smell of demon feet."

They walked down the tunnel for several yards, but still couldn't see or hear anything. After a few minutes, they found a large hole in the ground with several cables coming out of it. The cables were attached to pulleys above them.

Lobo checked the cables, but even with Devon's help, he couldn't get them to move. He turned to the Scribe. "Vampie, can you fly down and see if there's another way through? Our hands would probably burn if we had to slide down these things."

"I'll transform you," Devon said.

Vampie waved her off. "I think I have these Earth creatures down."

Vampie transformed into a bat without the Cherub's help and shot down the hole. A few minutes later, Lobo and Devon heard a buzzing sound as Vampie appeared in his normal form, standing on a platform.

"How's this?" he asked.

"Excellent," Lobo replied. "They set up an elevator. It's quiet."

"It's quieter because these cables are similar to the mite cables Baron was using," Vampie explained. "Different mites, similar result."

"Was anyone down there?" Lobo asked.

"I didn't see anything."

They eased down the elevator for several hundred feet before reaching the bottom. The place was still empty, but another tunnel was ahead. They moved through, passing mounds of loose soil. They soon reached an area filled with several machines that looked like mini riding lawn mowers, but with metallic round objects attached to the front.

"What are those?" Lobo asked.

Vampie reached into a machine and felt the handles. "Digging vehicles. I used to drive older models. Those circles in the front let out beams of heat and energy that can cut through rock and earth. Much more efficient than Earth drills."

Devon's head snapped to the side. She raised her finger to her lips. "I hear something."

Vampie's ears twitched. "Yes, I hear it now. Something's breathing."

"A Korindian, maybe?" Lobo asked.

"No, the smell would have been worse," Devon replied.

Vampie transformed and flew deeper into the tunnel and came right back. "There are Barna guarding another tunnel."

"How many?" Devon asked.

"I saw three of them."

They used their stealth skills to move closer. Lobo heard the Barna's high pitched conversation, which sounded like a cross between a bird's singing chirp and an eagle's screech.

The three hid behind one of the digging machines and were able to see the demons. "It's unusual to see Barna as the first level of defense," Devon whispered. "Korindians are much more disciplined."

"Maybe Dukane needed them to help with whatever he's really planning," Lobo said.

"True," she replied. "Plus, if they're guarding the Eye of the Traveler, they'd probably want something that will kill first, reason later."

That didn't make Lobo or Vampie feel any better.

"There's no other way in," Devon said. "We have to go through them."

Lobo reached into his pocket for his folded staff. His hand shook as he extended it.

Devon grasped his trembling hands to hold them steady. "This isn't like last time, Lobo. You have me."

Vampie transformed to his normal self. "I will assist in any way I can."

Lobo looked at them and smiled as he felt the shaking stop.

"It's time for the Freaksome Threesome to get loco on some demons."

CHAPTER EIGHTEEN:
AN EYE FOR TRUTH

"Lead the way, Lobo," Devon said. "Even if you're scared, don't let them see it."

Lobo gripped his staff and spun it. He stepped forward and walked toward the guards.

The Barna were scuffling with each other.

"Excuse me," Lobo's voice cracked. He cleared his throat and continued. "Excuse me, but we need to get to the tunnel behind you. I have my hall pass."

The Barna looked up, and without hesitating two of them rushed Devon and Vampie. The third moved cautiously toward Lobo.

Devon sped toward the Barna in front of her and dove to the ground. She kicked it in the face as it reached down to try and grab her.

The second demon laughed as it zoomed at Vampie. It wrapped its claws around the Scribe's neck. Vampie was trembling, but pulled out his Finger Quills and squirted ink into the Barna's eyes. It dropped him as Devon rushed past and smacked the blinded Barna with her hands clasped into one big fist.

"Vampie," Lobo said. "Head into the tunnel. We need to know if the Eye and the map are actually there or if we're just wasting our time."

Lobo's Barna attacked as he finished his sentence. It sped forward, cocked its arm back and struck, but Lobo ducked and spun, flipping his staff up to block the clawed fingers. The Barna chirped and kept slicing at its young enemy, but Lobo blocked each swipe and then struck it across the face, making it jump back. The Barna screamed and tried a different attack. It ran full speed and jumped in the air. Lobo swung his staff sideways but missed as the Barna tucked and rolled and came up with a swift kick to the stomach. Lobo couldn't move as the kick knocked the wind out of him.

The Barna bared its teeth and extended its claws as it rushed at its injured prey.

Lobo exhaled as he finally caught his breath. He swiped the staff and smacked the Barna, knocking it sideways. The force jarred the staff loose and it flew in the opposite direction. The Barna was back on its feet before the staff hit the ground. There was no way for Lobo to recover his weapon in time. The Barna stood over him, savoring the moment before its final strike. It revealed its full set of teeth and snapped its head down to bite Lobo's neck, but something smashed it from behind before it could finish.

Lobo was startled and blinded as dust blew into his face. He heard a thump as he rubbed his eyes and saw the Barna knocked out beside him. Large pieces of a shattered stone were by its head.

Devon jumped on the Barna and slammed her hands against its chest.

"Is it dead?" Lobo asked.

"No, but I've suspended its heartbeat and blood flow.

They'll be out for several hours."

Lobo saw the other two Barna a few feet away, face down and unconscious.

"Thanks for saving me. You could have jumped in a little sooner, though."

"You were doing okay. Much better than last time."

Vampie emerged from the tunnel. "It's here. Hurry." He scurried back.

"We're fine, Vampie," Lobo said in a sarcastic voice as he stood up. "Thanks for asking."

The opening led to one last room. The walls had hand and claw marks where the final digs must have taken place. In the far end of the small room, Lobo and Devon saw the Eye. It looked like an ice sculpture and was about a foot high. It was made up of two snake-like forms that twisted around each other, forming a thick handle. The top was a spiny ball with a round opening like an eyeball in the center. Golden ore was inside and a sharp white light shot from the eyeball to the ground, revealing a three-dimensional set of flat, odd shaped formations.

"What is that?" Lobo asked.

"It's a celestial map of the realms," Vampie replied. He pointed to one of the objects that was glowing. "The map is pointing to Osidian."

"That's Osidian? It doesn't look like Earth."

"They aren't round like your planets, Lobo," Vampie explained. "This is telling us Osidian is the destination, but I don't know how to find the exact spot."

"The Ultimate Brain said you just had to ask for what you seek, remember?" Devon said.

"You mean talk to it?" Lobo asked.

"Yes, and I think you should be the one to do it, Lobo."

Lobo cleared his throat and faced the Eye. "Dear Eye, sorry to disturb you. How are you today?"

"I don't think it has feelings, Lobo," Devon said. "Just treat it like a computer."

Lobo nodded. "Eye of the Traveler, where is the Dreaming Soul?"

Neither the Eye nor the map changed at first, but after a few seconds the Eye hissed softly and the map zoomed in on a high-level view of Osidian.

Lobo realized he had to be more precise. "Eye, please pinpoint the Dreaming Soul."

The Eye zoomed in further and they were able to see trees and animals roaming free. The Eye stopped on a structure they all recognized.

"It's in the High Council's chambers," Devon said. "We need to be there."

Lobo thought for a second. "The Ultimate Brain said if the Eye was disturbed before you found whatever you were looking for, that object would be gone."

"So if we take out the ore," Devon said, "then the Dreaming Soul will disappear."

"Then what are we waiting for?" Vampie asked as he reached for the Eye.

"Wait!" Devon said a moment too late. Vampie was struck by an invisible shield protecting the map and was thrown hard against the tunnel's side.

Lobo rushed to Vampie's side. "Are you okay?"

Vampie's head snapped up. "I should have known they would have protected it."

"It's a strong demon protection spell," Devon said. "It should protect it from just about anything. That explains why they left the Barna to guard it."

A large chunk of dirt fell on Vampie's face and some trickled into his mouth, making him cough. More dirt started falling and the ground shook.

"The shock from the blast must have rattled the

tunnels," Lobo said. "We need to get out of here."

Vampie jumped to his feet and they ran out as more soil fell around them. They moved down the tunnel and heard a deep bellow.

"Oh, no," Lobo said. "I think water broke through."

Devon focused on the sound. "You're right, and it's coming fast."

Lobo scanned the area. "There's no way out."

"There has to be," Devon said. "They would have made an alternate escape route in case of a cave-in. Even demons aren't that careless."

Vampie transformed into a bat and soared off, looking for another exit. Devon and Lobo ran in opposite directions, looking for any type of opening.

"There," Lobo shouted, pointing to an indentation on one of the side walls. The dirt was falling toward the center of it. "There has to be a hole under that."

The bellow turned into a louder roar.

Devon dashed toward the sinking hole and started digging with her hands. Lobo jumped beside her and helped.

"It's filled in too deep," Devon said. "The water will be here any second."

The sound of the approaching sea was overtaken by a loud beeping noise. They turned to see a bright light coming at them and saw that it was the overhead beam of a digger. Vampie was behind the wheel. "Get in!"

Lobo and Devon didn't hesitate. "Do you know what you're doing?" Lobo asked.

"It's been awhile, but I guess we'll find out what I still remember."

The water burst into the chamber just as the tip of the digger's drill hit the hole.

"Mouthpieces!" Devon yelled.

They slapped them in their mouths as the digger shot through the escape tunnel. The digger kept charging as they were engulfed by the weight of the water. After a few more feet, the soil gave way and the force of the water shot them into the sea like a whale expelling air through its blowhole.

The digger flipped and twisted, throwing Lobo from the vehicle. He panicked as he started sinking. Devon swam down and reached for him, but he smacked her across the face as he flapped his arms and knocked her back. He froze long enough for Devon to grab him and lead him back to the ship. Vampie was swimming ahead of them.

As soon as the water drained out of the hatch, Lobo spit out his mouthpiece and struggled to catch his breath. "That wasn't fun. I'm sorry I hit you, Devon."

"I know you didn't mean to. It's not like I needed my nose, anyway."

"We need to get back," Lobo said as he flipped on his communicator. "Baron, are you there?" All they heard was static.

"We've lost communication. We have to get to Osidian."

"Great. We can't use the Supershot and the portals are blocked," Devon said. "We need to dream travel."

"Then we need to get to the surface and find a baby," Lobo said. "Let's head to a beach."

"We have to conceal the Supershot," Devon said. "How do we move this thing without Baron?"

Vampie stared at the console of buttons and levers. "It has manual controls. I think I can figure this out. Hold on, I don't want to send us firing like a rocket again."

Vampie tried different controls until the Supershot started drifting. Within a few minutes, the vehicle surfaced near some large rocks.

"The beach should be close," Lobo said. He and Devon got out of the hatch. Vampie sent the Supershot underwater and then followed them out in his Chihuahua form.

The three moved from the rocks onto the nearby beach. There were nervous groups of people chatting and several swimmers returning to shore.

"That had to have been a quake," they heard a woman say as they walked by.

They saw several children playing with buckets and shovels, oblivious to the excitement around them. The trio moved toward them.

Devon stomped her foot into the sand. "No babies."

"Angel," a small voice said. A toddler, no more than three years old, was pointing at Devon. The child turned towards the woman behind him. "Mama, she angel."

"I have an idea," Devon whispered to her companions.

Devon walked towards the child and his mother.

"Excuse me, but my friend and I are trying to learn some magic tricks. Will you be our audience so we can practice?"

The woman turned toward the child. "You want to see some magic, Joey?"

Joey clapped his hands. "Magic!"

"I need a volunteer for this one. I need someone to pretend they're asleep."

Joey's eyebrows creased and he stared at her but didn't move.

"She wants you to go night-night," the mother said.

"Night-night?" Devon said.

"It's baby talk," Lobo said from behind her. "Something he can understand."

"Yes. Ni-night," Joey replied. He lay down on the sand, closed his eyes and pretended to snore.

Devon smiled at the Mom. "He's really good at this. Now for the trick. It's a disappearing act, but don't worry. It's all done with mirrors."

Devon held out her hand and blew the sand into Joey's face, turning his snores real.

Lobo put one hand on Devon's back and the other on Vampie's head. Devon quickly set her hands on Joey and they faded to the sound of Joey's mom clapping.

CHAPTER NINETEEN: FINAL ARRIVAL

The three appeared on Osidian near the flight training grounds. Devon's hands were on the head of an animal sleeping in the grass that looked like a cross between a weasel and a cat.

"Is Joey going to be okay?" Lobo asked.

"He'll be fine, Mama Lobo," Devon said. "He should be awake by now."

Lobo looked down at the weasel cat. "What is that?" he asked.

Vampie reached down to pet it. "A baby fornuk."

"You can jump on animal's dreams, too? Wait, animals can dream?"

"Everything's connected in the celestial realms, Lobo."

Vampie interrupted. "Where is everyone?" Except for the light rustling of tree leaves, it was silent. "That's a bad sign. We need to go."

They ran toward the High Council headquarters and didn't see a single creature along the way.

"Where could everyone have gone?" Devon's question

wasn't answered until they reached the top of the last hill.

Several hundred Osidianites were amassed around the steps below the council headquarters. Devon rushed ahead of her companions and stopped near a group of Fliers. Lobo recognized two of them as the flight instructors Kai and Joran.

"Kai, what's happening?" Devon asked.

Kai smirked. "Hey guys, Devon's returned. I heard you had an assignment on Earth. Didn't take them long to kick you out."

Devon grabbed Kai's shirt. "Just tell me what's happening."

Kai twisted her hand off him and turned back to his friends.

Joran stepped forward. "It's good to see you safe, Devon. The council called an emergency meeting and evacuated all non-council members. No one's sure what's going on, but they said we needed to leave for our own safety. Everyone's waiting to see what's happened."

"We need to get up there."

"I don't think you've become a council member since I last saw you," Kai said. "Unless they designated an official pet."

Devon cocked her arm back but Lobo grabbed her. "We don't have time. Is there any way in?"

"No. They disable the stairway entrance when they call an emergency meeting."

"Can't you ride a dream wave in?"

"No," Devon said. "There are no other passages to the council chambers and they would have closed the portals, but I think I know a way. Stay here."

Devon blended into the crowd, then reappeared a few minutes later, pulling another creature by its hand.

"Follow me," she said and led them away from the

crowd.

"Lobo and Vampie, this is Kino. He's a Phalene."

Kino waved one of his four scaly hands.

"Hello, Kino," Lobo said. "I don't understand, Devon. How can he help us?"

"Adult Phalenians have the ability to teleport," Vampie explained. "Anywhere."

Lobo, Devon and Vampie smiled at the unsuspecting Kino.

"Where do you want to go?" Kino said in a timid voice.

"Just outside the council chambers would be perfect," Devon said.

"Devon, you know that is not possible. We have been ordered to leave."

"The council is being attacked."

"And you know this for sure?"

"Not exactly, but all our evidence points to it."

Kino shook his head. "I would be violating the law, and you aren't even certain."

Devon grew agitated. "Kino, do you know who this boy is?"

"No, I do not."

"This is Jeremiah Coronado, the Grey Wolf's son. I'm helping him. We've done our own detective work and everything we've seen tells us the council is being attacked right now. Just teleport us there. You don't have to come. If we're wrong, I'll take the blame."

Kino gulped, almost swallowing his thin tongue. "If he is truly the son of Coronado, then you have my confidence."

Kino's bald, pointy head started to quiver. He grabbed Devon and Lobo's hands, and Devon grabbed Vampie. Kino's eyes flashed and the trio disappeared.

They reappeared a few feet from the council's

chambers, surrounded by three dead Sentraelian Guards. They recognized the screaming voice that echoed around them.

"You will tell me where the Dreaming Soul is!" Dukane said. "The Eye showed me that it was in this room."

Lobo snuck into the chamber and hid behind a pillar with his companions right behind. The room was filled with more than fifty Barna and Korindians. The council members were all on their knees as Dukane paced back and forth before them.

Lobo stared at Dukane for a long moment. He thought of his father in the hospital and his mother burning in the fire.

"That man killed my mother."

Devon scanned the room. "There are so many."

Lobo stood up. "I'm going to stop him right now."

Devon pulled him back down. "Lobo, calm down. We need to be smart about this. You're not going to stop him this way. Remember what happened with the Korindians."

He took a step forward. "I don't care."

Devon pulled him down and slapped him across the head. "What would the Grey Wolf do?"

Lobo froze. Devon hit hard. He felt his breathing ease a little as he thought of his father and snapped back to reality. "You're right. Lost myself for a moment."

"Glad to have you back. Now what?"

He thought as he rubbed his temple. "Is there a way to open the front gates and get the steps working again?"

"Yes," Devon replied. "There's a control room near the main entrance."

"Vampie, do you know where it is?"

Vampie nodded.

"Get to the booth and get the stair's running. Bring as much help as you can."

"We won't get any assistance," Devon said. "We're a peaceful world, remember? Sentrael provides protection to all of the celestial realms. For any other race, killing another creature or going to war without an official declaration can mean banishment to a demon realm forever."

"Vampie, tell them that the son of the Grey Wolf is asking for their help and that the fate of all the celestial realms is at stake."

Vampie rushed out.

Lobo and Devon moved to the next pillar.

Dukane stood in front of Alina.

"My patience is spent, council. I will start killing you one at a time until someone tells me where it is. I'll start with your mighty queen."

Dukane pulled a sword from his side and raised it inches from Queen Alina's face.

CHAPTER TWENTY: MEET AND GREET

Lobo stood up, ready to jump, but Devon pulled him back down and pointed.

Another council member was standing. "I will tell you where it is," he said. "Leave the rest of the council alone."

Dukane lowered his sword and moved toward the councilman. "You had better not be wasting my time. You're an Elidian, are you not? What's your name?"

"I am Geonique, council representative from the water realm of Elidia." Geonique had black marble skin and two thin strands of flesh hanging from the side of his head stretched down to his waist.

"Where is the Dreaming Soul, Elidian?"

"Guarantee me that you will spare the rest of the council's lives."

"I will guarantee their safety if you give me what I want."

Geonique pointed to his chest. "It is here."

"In your body?"

"Yes, hidden between my two hearts."

"Impressive," Dukane said. "Any telepathic scans would pick up your heartbeats or your own soul instead."

Geonique started to speak when Dukane shoved his sword through the councilman's torso so far that his fist entered the wound. The Elidian fell to his knees as several pints of clear water and blue blood spilled from the cut.

Dukane twisted his hand inside Geonique's chest and his fist popped back out, gripping a pointy object.

"The Dreaming Soul," Dukane said as Geonique's lifeless body fell to the ground with the sword still inside him.

"You said you wouldn't harm us," Queen Alina protested.

"I said I would harm no other council member, and so long as none of you try to stop me, I'll keep my word. This was the last piece I needed."

Dukane pulled a cloth from inside the jacket he was wearing and wiped off the Dreaming Soul, revealing a cristalinium protective casing. It was shaped like an icicle with a round ball in the center. It emitted a brilliant blue glow.

"Bring me the King's Chalice and the blood," Dukane said, holding his gaze on the Soul.

From the crowd, a woman in a black business suit stepped out, holding a large golden chalice in her hands.

Devon tapped Lobo's shoulder and pointed. "I think that's Dukane's office receptionist."

The woman set the chalice on the ground, then turned and snapped her fingers to someone behind her. A Korindian stepped forward and handed her a small case. She took out five small vials and poured their contents into the chalice.

"I have the blood of five of the demon realms. I need only the final one. Nora Lia, my lovely assistant, will you please take your natural form?"

The Barna and the Korindians yelled in encouragement. Nora Lia turned toward them, revealing her perfect haircut and pretty smile. Her smile grew wider as she raised her hands to cover her face. She moved her hands apart. Half of her face was the same, but the left side changed. The new half revealed a chapped, strung together facial structure without a smooth patch of skin. One eye turned completely black. Her left hand's fingers turned into skinless pointy digits with sharp ends.

"Nora Lia, of the demon realm of Painsure, I ask that you add the final ingredient to the mix," Dukane said.

Nora raised her arms high. Her transformed arm looked like it came from a body that had died years ago. She used her normal hand to squeeze her scarred, bony arm, allowing thin drops of blood to fall into the chalice. The mixed blood changed from dark red to dark green and back again, then let out a black cloud of smoke.

"He's going to summon the Anointer," Devon said.

Lobo stood tall, still behind the pillar. "We have to stop this."

"How?"

"Wait for Vampie. I have to at least try and distract him."

Lobo remembered the words his father had spoken to him. Channel fear. Channel anger. Powerful allies.

Lobo closed his eyes, took in a deep breath and stepped out into the open. He ran toward the back of the guards. His chest pounded and he could feel his heart beating in his throat with every stride. As Dukane reached down to lift the chalice, Lobo yelled, "Put that down!"

A Korindian turned and readied for Lobo, who pulled out his staff and extended it without stopping. Two more Korindians and a Barna moved next to each other, forming a wall of defense. Lobo ran faster and swung his staff backward, prepared to strike. Instead, he shoved the end of the staff onto the lead Korindian's foot and catapulted himself over the guards, landing only a few steps from Dukane and the King's Chalice. Lobo eyed the chalice and sliced his staff toward it, but Dukane caught the staff with his bare hand.

"I don't know who you are, but you have no place here."

"I can't let you do this," Lobo said.

Dukane took a better look at him. "You're not from Osidian. What is a human boy doing here? Who are you?"

Lobo took a defensive stance and held his staff in front of him. A few guards stepped forward, but Dukane waved them back.

"Answer me." Dukane's booming voice echoed throughout the chamber.

Lobo's face was hard and his gaze was focused on Dukane. "My name is Jeremiah Coronado. My family calls me Lobo."

Dukane lowered his guard for a moment, then took a step toward the boy. Lobo raised his staff, but Nora Lia snuck up behind him and snatched the weapon from his hands and threw it aside. Dukane grabbed Lobo's jaw. Lobo took a bare-knuckled swing, but Dukane blocked it without effort.

Dukane studied his face and then noticed the wolf medallion with the glowing eyes. "The son of the Grey Wolf lives. You have your father's intensity, young one, but you also have his faults. You've tried to fight an enemy you have no chance of defeating."

"I can stop you. I can kill you," Lobo said.

"Big words from such a small Coronado." Dukane turned toward the council. "Queen Alina, you knew this boy was alive?"

Alina turned her face and didn't respond.

"It makes sense. Your cowardly race won't face me, so you bring a human to pick up his father's pieces."

Dukane dropped his grip, then backhanded Lobo across the cheek with his clenched fist, sending him sliding across the floor as the guards cheered.

"You made a bad choice for your champion, Queen," Dukane said before turning toward his guards. "Tie him down and have him take the place of the Elidian," Dukane ordered.

Two Korindians tied up Lobo and made him kneel next to the dead councilman.

"This is fitting, Lobo Coronado. In fact, it's somewhat of a pleasant surprise. I'll have the son of my worthiest enemy see me rise to heights that his father could never imagine."

"This isn't something my father would have wanted."

"It's because he was cursed with mediocrity. Greatness was never in his grasp."

"My father. . ."

"Speak no more," Dukane said, drawing a small dagger from his side. He moved toward Lobo. "Speak no more, or I'll remove your tongue."

Lobo didn't flinch but kept silent.

Dukane walked back toward the chalice and lifted it toward his lips. He sipped the black blood, savoring each drop. Dukane started shaking and grabbed at his chest and stomach. The remaining blood in the chalice started to expand and some spilled out onto the floor. The liquid thickened and spread into a bubbling pool. The bubbles burst as a mass rose out of the center of the blackness.

CHAPTER TWENTY-ONE:
A ROYAL BATTLE

The Anointer rose through the blood. It kept rising until it stood almost twelve feet tall. Its head was as large as a boulder and it had a snout and two deep, green eyes. Its upper body was pure muscle mass and it stood facing Dukane with its arms appearing to be crossed. As it turned, Lobo realized that its hands were fused together in one shared fist.

The Anointer whispered, yet his voice could be heard by all. "Summoner, state your business."

Dukane was unable to speak. The Anointer's eyes grew brighter and Dukane's body started to rise into the air. Although Dukane was a tall man, he looked tiny floating next to the monster before him. Dukane rose until his face was only inches from the Anointer.

"State your business."

Dukane pulled up the Dreaming Soul. "Complete your task."

Dukane raised the Soul's pointed casing but was interrupted by a loud commotion at the back of the room.

Devon and Vampie rushed in with a large crowd of Osidianites behind them. The demonites were outnumbered, but they took their defensive stances and prepared to fight. Devon was several steps ahead of the group before she realized everyone behind her had stopped. She turned toward the crowd.

"They will kill the council and kill us all. We have to fight."

Devon rushed up to the Korindian nearest her and struck it hard. It wasn't expecting such a large blow from such a small Cherub and fell on its back. Three other Korindians attacked. Devon kicked one on its stubby knee and it slammed into a nearby pillar, cracking it. Another guard hit Devon in the stomach. She slammed into the cracked pillar and it fell on top of her.

Vampie rushed to try and lift the shattered stone. It didn't budge and no one else came to his aid.

Devon saw a group of familiar faces. "Kai, Joran, please help Vampie. Help us fight!"

Kai started to take a step forward but stopped. "I'm sorry, Devon," Kai said. "We could be banished."

"We may not have a world to be banished from, you idiot!"

Dukane fell back to the ground as the Anointer focused on the interruption. "Don't trouble yourself," Dukane assured. "Other than the Cherub, no one else will attack. This is a peaceful world that does not believe in violence."

"Council!" Devon yelled. "We can't just let them destroy us!"

Dukane walked back to Alina.

"This is their queen. Even with her own realm of Osidian in danger, she will just watch her people die and her world fall."

Dukane pulled his dagger from his side and slid it

around her throat.

"Queen Alina," Devon said. "Tell them to defend themselves."

A Korindian kicked her.

The crowd stood still.

Lobo struggled to stand up. "Osidian, Dukane will kill your Queen and then kill your families. On Earth, we've had wars just to defend one country. This is your entire world."

Dukane motioned to a guard and the Korindian punched Lobo in the stomach, sending him back to his knees.

Lobo grunted but ignored the pain. "Please, Queen Alina, tell them to fight."

"You won't do that, will you, Queenie?" Dukane taunted. "How pathetic."

Dukane slammed the handle of his dagger across Alina's face. The crowd gasped, but no one moved to help their leader.

Alina gathered herself and got back to her knees. Her lip was bleeding. Dukane grabbed the back of her head. "What kind of race won't even try to defend itself? Are you so concerned with sin that you don't even value your life?"

"The good thing about the system," Alina whispered, "is that you can sin now and ask for forgiveness later." The queen bit Dukane's wrist and turned to the crowd as he jumped back in pain.

"People of Osidian, I ask you to emulate the angels in heaven when they are called into battle. Defend yourselves against those that would destroy your world."

The crowd yelled and rushed the guards. Kai and Joran knocked down the Korindians standing over Devon and helped Vampie lift the shattered pillar.

Dukane rushed back to the Anointer. "Ignore them. We

still have time." He lifted the Dreaming Soul, but he was slammed by Lobo, who had gotten to his feet and hopped as fast as he could, throwing his body against Dukane. Dukane fell, but jumped back on his feet and hit Lobo with the Soul's casing.

Lobo tried to get back up, but Dukane was standing over him with his dagger drawn. Above Dukane's head, Lobo saw Kai flying above the crowd, holding an angry Cherub in mid-air.

Devon pulled her arm back and threw a piece of stone just as Kai shifted his flight path. The stone hit Lobo on top of his head and knocked him back down again.

Dukane looked up at Devon. "My cowgirl pickpocket. To think I liked you."

He laughed in Lobo's face. "Your own help may be more dangerous to you than I am. I have a ritual to complete. Once I have been anointed, you'll be my first victim. I'm sure you'll be happy to join your mother and father."

Dukane returned to the Anointer. He slammed the bottom of the Dreaming Soul's pointed casing into its body. The casing's blue shimmer dimmed and the center of the Anointer's chest glowed blue as the Soul transferred into him.

"Charge them," Devon yelled at Kai.

Kai flew straight at the Anointer and Dukane, but the Anointer simply turned his head and shot a bright electric flash at the pair, knocking them through the top floor's railings. The Anointer then turned back to Dukane as if nothing had happened.

Lobo saw Devon stand up and brush herself off. She took another stone in her hand and scraped it against the marble like railings. She repeated the process with a few more strikes and was yelling something at Kai. The flight instructor picked her up and hovered over the fighting crowd.

Lobo got to his knees and tried to shuffle toward Dukane to distract him.

Devon threw a sharpened stone with her full force, but Lobo knew she was off target as soon as she let it go. It buzzed by his head and struck right between his bound wrists, cutting the cord. Lobo looked up and Devon gave him a thumbs up sign. He nodded in thanks as he freed his legs and turned toward his target.

The Dreaming Soul's container was empty. Dukane dropped the container and it shattered on the ground. The Anointer's entire chest glowed so bright that the bones in his torso were visible.

"Now," Dukane said, his voice trembling with excitement. "The blood of every demon realm runs through my veins and the Dreaming Soul has mixed inside you. I ask that you anoint me, for I am worthy to rule."

The Anointer held up his fused hands. He pulled them apart, revealing a long, sharp claw on each fist that looked like unicorn horns.

"Kneel, human," the Anointer ordered.

Dukane bowed down. The Anointer set each claw against Dukane's throat. Dukane raised his neck as the Anointer slammed the tip of each claw through his skin.

Lobo shot himself at Dukane with every ounce of speed he could gather, tackling him from the side. Dukane fell with Lobo and the holes in his neck splattered blood as they separated from the Anointer's claws.

Dukane got back to his feet, but almost lost his balance. "If now is the time you wish to die, let's get on with it."

Dukane swung two big punches at Lobo, but he was ready for him. Although Lobo was weaponless, he moved fast, forcing Dukane to slam his hand into the wall.

"Stay still and fight, coward!"

Dukane fell on his face as Devon hit him from behind. He tried to fight back, but Devon's strikes and his wasted energy were too much for him in his weakened state.

"Anointer, as your Summoner, I command you to destroy the human's companion. Kill everyone if you must, but not the boy. Leave him within inches of his life so that I may be the one to take it from him."

The Anointer grabbed Devon before she could turn. It flung her across the room and she smashed into a wall.

The Anointer stepped toward her.

"Leave her alone!" Lobo yelled.

The demon kept moving. Lobo searched for his staff and saw it behind the large beast. He rushed toward the Anointer and threw himself on the ground, sliding through the creature's legs. It heard the rush of air and swung his claws, but Lobo slid too fast. He picked up his staff and jumped to the side, striking the Anointer across its stomach as he flew by. It turned its back toward Lobo, unaffected by the hit.

It took two long steps and took several large swings, but Lobo was able to use his speed to dodge each pass. He darted toward the Anointer and threw himself in the air with his staff, but the demon beast was fast, too. It struck Lobo in mid-air, knocking him against a fighting Korindian, which helped soften his landing.

"He's too strong, Lobo," Devon said. "You can't beat him with your fists or with your staff. Run before he kills you."

Lobo stood his ground as the Anointer approached. He held his staff up, although he knew it would be useless. As he tried to think of what to do next, he noticed an object that the monster was stepping over. The King's Chalice had remained in its position, undisturbed through all the madness.

Lobo was captivated by the chalice for a moment too long. The Anointer grabbed him and wrapped its huge hand around his body. Lobo felt the grip tighten and yelled as he heard something snap. As the fierce burst of pain on his side grew, a rush of air passed by his ears and the Anointer let go, dropping Lobo back to the ground.

Lobo opened his eyes and saw the Anointer grabbing its face. Devon had hit him in the eye with a stone.

"Get out of there!" Devon yelled.

Lobo, grabbing his side, winked at Devon and gave her a half smile. He lifted his staff again.

"Lobo, what are you doing?"

The Anointer was standing over him, ready for a final strike. Lobo raised his staff as if he were going to attack, but instead took off running past his opponent. He jumped over the chalice and dipped the tip of his staff into the mixed blood just as the Anointer caught his shoulder. In one swift motion, Lobo used the force of the Anointer's pull to flip around and jam the blood-stained staff into the demon's chest.

The demon's hard skin shattered like glass as the staff penetrated him.

The creature pushed Lobo back, making him trip over Dukane, who was still trying to gather his strength. It let out a bloodcurdling banshee scream that shook the walls of the chamber as its chest burst open. The Anointer's body broke into chunks that liquefied into dark pools of blood.

The remaining guards stopped as they realized Lobo had just defeated a monster they all feared. The Osidianites took advantage of the situation and within seconds, the last of the Korindians and Barna were beaten.

Kai and Joran freed the council as the crowd

surrounded Dukane and Lobo.

Dukane was still groggy but found enough strength to grab Lobo around the neck.

"How did you defeat the Anointer, Son of Coronado?" Dukane demanded as he pulled his dagger from his side. "How is that possible?"

"I'm not much of a fighter," Lobo answered. "I just thought of my father and how he would be using his detective skills and not his fists. Once I saw the chalice, I realized the blood had summoned the Anointer, so I figured that it might send him back."

Dukane shook his head in disbelief. "You will not take your father's place, Lobo Coronado. I can't have another one of you stopping me. I will end this right now."

"Cease," Alina's voice bellowed.

"Will you risk your lives and your principles for a human?" Dukane asked as he stuck the tip of his dagger against Lobo's throat.

"He is not just any human," Alina responded. "He is one of us."

"I have his destiny in my hands, Queen."

"You can't escape, Micah Dukane."

Dukane stepped back, pulling Lobo with him. Lobo grabbed Dukane's arm and pushed himself down, thrusting his head out of his grip. Dukane swung his blade, but the youngest Coronado was able to dodge the attack. Lobo jumped to his feet and faced his enemy.

"Had the Anointing ritual not weakened me, you would be just another dead Coronado," Dukane hissed.

"It's over, Dukane," Lobo said. "You've lost."

"It's only beginning, you ignorant little boy. What you don't realize is that I got exactly what I came for."

A loud screeching sound from above distracted everyone. Nora Lia was on the higher observation floor and leapt into the air. She flipped and twisted as she fell, pulling something from her side as she landed. She dashed through the crowd before anyone could react and squeezed the round object in her hand as soon as she reached Dukane. A loud explosion ensued as light and smoke spread from their location.

The pair disappeared.

CHAPTER TWENTY-TWO: RESOLUTIONS

Several hours later, it was hard to tell there had been a battle that day. The floors were clean and all the Korindians and Barna had been buried or arrested. Most of Osidian's citizens had been healed, but five had perished. This would bring celebrations the next day, as the inhabitants of Osidian knew that the souls of the departed were in a higher plane.

The only battle scars left in the council's chambers were the missing pillar and several holes in the wall, but they were already being repaired.

Lobo stood on a far side of the chamber holding up his shirt. Devon had her hands on the black bruise on his side.

"You have a cracked rib," she said. "It will heal, but the bruise will take a few days to disappear."

"I'll take that over a broken bone," Lobo said. "Thank you."

"Lobo," Alina's voice echoed. "We are convening a council meeting. Your presence is requested."

Lobo nodded. The council members appeared, taking

their seats. The only empty chair belonged to Geonique of Elidia.

Devon and Vampie joined their human companion as Osidianites gathered for the meeting.

"First, Lobo, I have a message for you," Alina said. A holographic picture appeared above the seated council.

"Hello, Grandfather," Lobo said.

"You've done well, Grandson. Dukane had everyone fooled except for you. The Zaan was just a distraction. While we were busy searching for the demon world where the ceremony was to be held, he used the extracted essence of a Phalene's teleportation power to get to Osidian. He has disappeared and we do not believe he is an immediate threat. The one thing I know for certain is that you are definitely your father's son."

"What about what he said to me?" Lobo asked. "He said he got what he wanted."

"We're not sure what he meant by that. Baron could use your help when you return. We have at least bought ourselves some time to find out his true intentions."

"Thank you for opening this world to me, Grandfather."

"You're welcome, Lobo." Cornelius bowed his head as his image disappeared.

"We owe you our lives, Lobo," Alina said. "I know that your mother and father would have been proud."

"None of this could have happened without Devon and Vampie."

"Yes, your unusual crew. Vonqua the Vampire, we have looked over your preliminary notes and you have exceeded our expectations. The level of detail will help us chronicle the events that have transpired. I request that you remain Scribe for Lobo, as his journey has just begun."

Vampie stopped writing as his face beamed. "It would

be an honor, my Queen. And if you don't mind, I think I prefer my new nickname."

"Noted, Vampie. And as for you Devon the Cherubim, we have had a lively discussion about you. Although we have a few protesters, there is no doubt that you proved yourself worthy. You have been granted first level Guardianship. You will be granted an evolved wing set and will have your choice of any human infant, which is what you've always wanted, correct?"

Devon's lip curled. "I've already got my assignment. Lobo needs me more than any drooling baby."

Alina smiled. "As you wish, Devon. The three of you do make an excellent team."

"I don't mean to question you, Queen," Devon continued. "But I am curious about something. Why did you pick me?"

"The very thing that has hindered you on Osidian is a necessary trait on Earth. Your lack of respect for authority and willingness to ignore the rules to get the job done were critical to your mission. From that perspective, you were more than qualified."

Alina set her hand on Devon's shoulder. The new Guardian twisted as her back started to itch. Her wings spread, growing a few inches longer. She stretched them slowly, enjoying every movement.

"Lobo, we have assigned Vampie as your Scribe and Devon as your guardian, but I believe I am exhibiting rude behavior by assuming that you would continue. I have an important question to ask. The High Council would like to offer you the place of your father. We want you to be our own guardian, our Celestial Detective. If you choose not to accept, we will understand and be eternally grateful for what you've done here today."

Lobo paused for a few seconds. "I don't think that I can

ever fill my father's shoes."

Devon and Vampie lowered their heads in disappointment.

"But if I can just be half the person he was, I think I'll be okay. It would be an honor, council. As long as my friends are by my side, I know we can finish this."

The crowd buzzed with excitement.

"Lobo, I am aware that this is far from over until we find Micah Dukane. However, you did save our world. On behalf of myself and the High Council, is there anything we can do for you? Please don't be shy."

Lobo didn't reply right away. He glanced toward the end of the row of council members.

"There is one thing, but I'm not sure if it would be rude to ask."

Devon punched him in the arm. "Go ahead and be rude. You earned this, Amigo."

Lobo exhaled deeply. "I'd like to ask you, Thornos, if I can visit my memories one more time."

Thornos stood up and walked toward Lobo.

"It would be a privilege."

"Please, follow me," Alina asked. "I'd like to give Lobo some privacy."

Lobo and Thornos followed Alina into her private quarters.

"Take all the time you need," she said as she left the room.

Lobo spent the next few hours inside the memories of his mother and father. He didn't choose to see the moments of a great hero detective or the many accomplishments of a successful councilwoman. Instead, he watched the Coronado family spending time together. He visited his birth and saw his father and mother hold each other as they looked into the face of their newborn son. He saw his first birthday party, where his mother stuck a party hat on her nose just to make Lobo laugh. His favorite memory was seeing Sebastian chase him down a hill until he leapt into his mother's arms, squealing with delight. The images made Lobo feel as if his soul was already in heaven.

For a brief moment in time, Lobo Coronado was complete.

ABOUT THE AUTHOR

Manuel Ruiz[3] is a life-long Texan, born in the town of Alice and raised in nearby Robstown, the birthplace of Texas Hold 'Em. He earned his Bachelor of Science degree in Math/Computer Science from Texas A&M University - Kingsville.

Manuel currently lives in Round Rock where he balances his time around his family, his PlayStation and giving the characters in his head something interesting to do.

To learn more about Manuel Ruiz[3] and his books, please visit his website. Subscribe to Manuel's newsletter to receive all the latest updates!

www.manuelruiz3.com

FREE STORIES!

Subscribe to Manuel's e-mail list to get three FREE short stories. Go to his website to sign up!

www.manuelruiz3.com

Leave an online review for *Lobo* and receive two additional stories FREE! Just send a link/screenshot of your review to:

manuel@manuelruiz3.com

Also available from Manuel Ruiz³

The Dead Club

Social Media

Facebook:
www.facebook.com/ManuelRuizThree

Twitter:
@ruizman

Special Thanks

To my first team of Beta Readers,
thank you for your invaluable input.

David Riskind
Michael Sawyer
Mari Molina
Belynda Chapa
Pam "PMoney" Marino
and my first reader,
Daisy Ruiz

Made in the USA
Charleston, SC
28 February 2017